I0458060

Dr. T Chronicles: Ocular Deception
© 2011 Torey Scott Irving

ISBN: **978-0615583266** TSI Publishing

Acknowledgements

First and foremost, I would like to thank my Lord and Saviour, Jesus Christ. Thank you for blessing me with the skills and talent to do what I do. Without you, I am nothing.

I also would like to thank my parents for always encouraging me and loving me no matter what. Momma, thank you so much for having a belt next to you to inspire me not to miss a spelling word (smiles).

Momma, without your love and support, I would still be writing for the heck of it. I love you way beyond what words can describe.

Dad, thanks for always being there for me and teaching me how to be a real man. You are my role model and my best friend. I often brag about you because I know in my heart that I'm one lucky man to be so blessed to have you as my father. I only hope to be half the man you are, thank you.

Also I would like to thank my twin sister, Latoya, for always believing in me, and my big brother, Marcus, for encouraging me as well. I want to send my thanks out to Rena Wright for helping me write, this book was born from a poem that I wrote and you challenged me to turn it into a book, thank you for the vision you see in me.

Thanks to The1Essence, my friend, my editor and book cover designer, I truly don't know how I could have come this far without you, thank you for everything that you have done and helped me with.

Also, I would like to thank everyone who believes in me and supports me, Kristie Elzey, L'Tenia James, Derek Stevenson for my cover and some of the people I work with. Thank you for taking the time out to preview my story and believing in what I write, you are my motivation.

I understand that this book is erotic, and what some people believe shouldn't be written, but trust me, everything that goes on in this book, is going on somewhere and if you are not a fan of erotic storytelling then please put my book down because it's obviously not for you to read.

Thank you to all my past relationships, I hold no negativity to any of you, without you, I wouldn't be here. I've been taught a plethora of things through my failures and I wish nothing but the best for you all, because you had a part in making me the man I am today, and it's a man I'm very proud to be, thank you.

Finally, I would like to give a special thanks to my wife, Shelba Irving. Thank you for the constant encouragement and love that you continue to show me. Thanks for understanding the long hours that I had to put into writing this book. You are my world and still to this day, I look at you in amazement. Never did I think that I could have everything I always wanted in a wife, but you proved me wrong.

You are everything I wanted that I thought no longer existed. If I missed anyone, please know it wasn't intentional. Thank you all!!

Dedication

This book is dedicated to everyone who believes in Love. It's dedicated to every woman who's had her heart broken, time and time again, but still have to courage to love again. And to every woman that seeks true love and to every man that treats women like the queens that they are. Yes, this book is erotic, but in the end, it's about love, so this book is dedicated to everyone who believes in Love.

"Love is in the risk that we take. We must not take for granted our journey of dealing with hurt from past loves, so we can truly appreciate arriving at our destination of our True Love"
Torey Irving

Chapter 1

"Thank you for that Dr. T.," Maria Gallegos said, putting stilettos back on those delectable feet. Hair pins dangled from her full pouty lips. She tried in vain to repair the havoc I reaped on her hair.

"Dr. T it's amazing how you know exactly where I need to be touched."

She removed the pins from her mouth, one by one, replacing each strand of hair that I pulled out. Her eyes closed and a look of ecstasy washed over her face.

"And the way your touch sends a…." Maria was interrupted. My next appointment was due soon after and I didn't have time for pillow talk.

"So Maria, you'll call me for your next appointment, right?"

"Yes Dr. T, but can I ask you a question?"

"Go for it."

"Um…How do you know what we need when you see us?

I mean, we call you to make an appointment and you never ask what it is we want."

"That's simple Maria. I'm Dr. T; I always know what you need. The ability to help women become receptive to love and all that it entails is a gift I don't question, like psychic ability or ESP."

"Dr. T, why aren't you married? Don't you want to be pleased or be loved so you could...?" I shook his head in frustration.

"Maria, don't question what can't be explained. Some things are better left a mystery. Just call me for your next appointment."

I glanced down at my watch, hoping she would realize that I had no more time for her. I couldn't just say shut up and go already.
I was known as a lover and couldn't disrespect any lady no matter how badly I got the urge to say something out of character.

Maria dropped her head looking up at me with bedroom eyes, silently pleading for a response.

She wanted more of Daddy Dick. She wanted to be more than just someone I felt I needed to please. That wasn't happening.

Her expression made it clear that my job wasn't complete. She smiled and spoke in a subdued tone, resigned to the fact it was time for her to leave.

"Ok Papi."

She bent over my desk to write out a check for the pleasure I had just bestowed upon her. Thick toned thighs peeked from beneath a knee length skirt that rode up on that entire ass to reveal the lips of her juicy pussy. My dick got hard immediately.

Her husband was a fool. That was more than enough for two men to handle. Maria was physically the perfect woman, thick in all right places, including her bank account. From my vantage point, I could see the amount of zeros on the check. It was well over usual and customary.

I long pressed the button on the intercom to notify my secretary to reschedule my appointments for the day. We had a system, one beep to rescue me from a client, two beeps to cancel everything for the day and

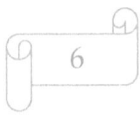

go home early because I was about to break somebody back up in here.

Maria slowly walked by and my scent clung to her moist skin, smelling like au de just been fucked. I couldn't let her walk away with questions about my personal life on her mind. Not me. The ladies left my office happy and I accepted nothing less.

I grabbed her hand and pulled her close to me. Her face was flushed and her eyes shone with excitement and pleasure, making her even more beautiful than usual. Or perhaps, it was the new air of confidence she held since our first appointment that made the difference.

"You really are beautiful Maria Gallegos," I whispered in her ear.

"You got me harder than Chinese arithmetic. When you bent over that table all I could think about was pushing up inside you again, and again, and again. Your pussy is addictive. I enjoy watching my dick plunge in and out, sliding between the cheeks of your fat ass.

When you grab me, and pull me in deeper, it makes it hard for me not to cum. Your thighs are luscious too, except I don't think anyone has ever taken the time to kiss you properly."

Maria opened her mouth to tell me something. Just as she did, I ran my tongue across her lower lip making her gasp at the intense pleasure. My begging mouth pressed against hers, taking little sips that did nothing to relieve her obvious need for intimacy.

Her breath came in tiny pants. She arched her neck, offering her mouth to me, begging me to take it without words, except she wasn't silent. Soft whimpers escaped her hungry mouth and refused to give in. There was no need to hurry because we had all day.

In desperation, she reached for me, wrapping her arms around my neck and pulling my mouth to hers. Our lips met in a passionate kiss and the more I kissed her, the more aggressive she got.

Maria melted against my chest, her body limp with desire. I then leaned her against the desk, kept clear for just such a reason.

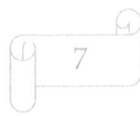

Our lips became emotionally and physically entwined for what seemed like an eternity. When I finally raised my lips from hers, we were both gasping for breath. She was honored and blessed to have my intimacy, but I ultimately felt that was more admiration than I deserved.

Why was I surprised? She was in love with me, just like all of the rest.

Maria gave all she had behind these closed doors. As a professional, I would gladly take it all and ask for more. She came to me to test her limits and expand her capacity for love and passion. As a man, it never failed to bother me how easily led women were.

Maria leaned back, her skirt rode above her waist, exposing her shaved pussy with the fat lips and sensitive clit. The thong she wore got lost in her ample derriere. It left nothing to the imagination.

Together we removed our clothes, leaving them in a pile on the floor. She stood in bra and panties, struggling to find ways to hide her curves from me, as if I cared. She crossed her arms over the soft round curve of her belly. Her face slightly turned from me.

"Look at me." I demanded.

Maria turned to face him.

"Put your hands down. I want to see you."

She put her hands down. The expression on her face wary, watching my reaction. I licked my lips to let her know she was about to get it. She smiled.

"Damn woman, you look delicious. Take off your bra and panties for me."

She rushed to get it done.

"No Maria! Take your time. Go slow." I said while turning on the Boise system. R. Kelly played in the background.

My dick throbbed and I wanted to take her. Instead, I pressed my mouth to her throat and nibbled, tasting the salty sweetness of her flesh. My mouth found the sensitive spot behind her ear and the place at the base of her throat where her pulse beat wildly.

"Please, Dr. T....please...." Maria moaned, her body moving like a snake, writhing in ecstasy.

My dick stroked up and down her thigh like a third hand, hard and demanding.

I slipped one arm beneath her, forcing her to arch her back. My other hand pulled her nipples to hard peaks. I took one puckered tip of nipple into my mouth and suckled gently, sending waves of pleasure crashing over her.

She trembled in my arms. My hands were magic, casting spells wherever I touched, and I touched her everywhere. I left a trail of wet kisses across her belly, stopping to dip into her navel. As my mouth moved down on her, my hands wandered up, rubbing thighs, sliding between them, sending tremors racing over her until she instinctively opened her legs to me.

I looked up at her. Her eyes were closed. I liked to watch. My dick hung heavy between my legs, throbbing and pulsating. Pre-cum oozed from the tip. My tongue explored the warm moist center of her. Oooos and aaaaahs spilled from Maria's mouth over the music. My spin cycle tongue worked her over, round and round, up and down.

"Tell me you want me Maria."

"Yes." she breathed.

"Say it. Tell me you want me."

"I....I want...I want Daddy Dick. I want to feel him inside me."

I came up from Mariaville, moving my body, warm and hard along the length of her.

My manhood was hard as wood, prodding against the ache I created in her pussy. She opened to me, lifting herself. Her sighs mingled with my moans when I entered her, filling her with my strength.

"Shit." Maria sighed low and sensual. Her need grew more intense with each stroke and thrust. I pumped deep in her belly to the rhythm of R. Kelly's, 'Seems Like You're Ready'.

"Please let me suck Mr. Good Dick," Maria moaned.

"Please...Please..."

I ignored her. Instead, I flipped her over and put legs on my shoulders and went deeper and deeper and deeper.

"Mmmm...Dr. T....Shit...I'm cumming.....I'm...."

I exploded in her womb. The Magnum condom kept my seed from spilling inside her.

Now once again, Maria had to fix her hair and put on her stilettos. While she was getting ready I asked sarcastically if she had any more questions for me.

"Yes." Maria answered.

"I appreciate what you do for me, but don't you want to be loved and pleased?"

Here we go again. "Maria?"

"Yes?"

"Call me if you need anything, ok?"

"Ok Papi."

She walked away. This time I didn't pull her back to me. Maria's questions still stayed with me. The truth was, there was one woman who loved me and pleased me and had plans of me as her only, or so she said. Then I found her in bed with someone else. I did everything that was physically, mentally and emotionally possible for this woman yet she claimed it wasn't enough for her and she didn't want me anymore. I loved too hard.

I read her, not to the point of being a mind reader, but a love reader. I guess she just needed an excuse out, but what this one woman did to me was accuse me of not being there for her, not loving her, not needing her and not wanting her. The sad thing is I believed this woman.

So I studied women's frustrations, body language and it got so detailed for me I knew something was wrong with them just by the way they blinked. Naturally, we're all fast blinkers, but I approached women who had a slow blink and something was always bothering them from what they told me.

Then I got to the point where I was too damn good at knowing what women want. Believing my past love, saying I didn't love her enough or please her enough, I made it my mission to make sure every woman I encounter is pleased, single or not. Sure, I would love to be loved and pleased and be married with kids, but knowing that a woman feels, needed, and wanted is more important to me.

So, what would it take for me to let someone please me and love me? I couldn't answer that, because I don't know. It'll happen when it's supposed to. For now, I give women what I think they want and I'm always right.

Some need love making, some simply need to be fucked, and some need affection or somebody to talk to and just listen. I never came across a woman that genuinely wanted to get to know about me and that's ok. I think if that woman ever comes along, then I'll be in love.

Chapter 2

"Hey Natalie girl, how you doing?" Natalie wiped her eyes.

"Wait......have you been crying?" Maria asked. "Naw Maria, I ain't been crying girl, what's up?"

"Come on Natalie what's wrong? It's obvious you've been crying, so tell me."

Natalie couldn't hold back her tears anymore. "I feel like a stupid idiot, crying like this in front of all these people in this restaurant." She broke down and sobbed.

"Fuck these people girl, they don't matter, now tell me. What's bothering you?"

"Maria, I just want to be loved. I'm a big girl and big girls are not in right now or will they ever be. I just want to be thought of, cared about, loved and

touched. No one gives me a second look and if they do, it's a look of disgust. I want someone to call me and say they were just thinking of me. I want someone to ask me how my day went and if there was anything I needed. I really want for someone to stop telling me I need to go work out, but actually help me work out and be with me when I work out." She said all that without taking a breath.

Maria laughed. "Damn girl, you want Jesus!"

Natalie tried to laugh and wiped her eyes.

"Girl, I want what you have, I want love."

Maria's mood changed. She took a sip of her apple martini.

"If what I got is love, then you definitely don't want it, trust me. It is definitely getting better though, all because of the Doc."

Natalie laughed a short and sarcastic snort.

"Damn, if love got you seeing a doctor, then you right, I don't want it."

Maria made a small sound of frustration, and then looked off in the distance.

"Girl, if only you knew. This man is a gift to all us women, seriously. Shit, I'm feeling him inside me now, or is it the apple martini?" She looked up again and to the side.

"Naw, I know this feeling, its Dr. T. He's not really a doctor, but he's known as Dr. T and fixes everything without you even telling him what's wrong."

Natalie laughed. "Ok, no more for you to drink cuz you tripping! Do you really think I'ma believe it's a nigga out there like that? You trippin for real!"

Maria took another sip of her martini. "Ok, if you are really down like you say and you really need love and all those things, I'm telling you that you need to call him and you won't even have to tell him what's wrong."

Maria fished in her purse and pulled out a card.

"Here is his number, call him and trust me when I say good things will come from this for you. He is all about pleasing and don't want to be pleased. His goal is making sure you feel like a woman should feel. His touch is so powerful he makes my man's touch powerful."

Natalie's eyes got big. "Word?"

"Yeah girl. He does this with his dick." Maria smiled wickedly.

"Mr. Good Dick as I call it. I'm telling you, this in no average dick. I feel Mr. Good Dick pulsating inside me and it talks to me.

Dr. T don't even have to say a word. Mr. Good Dick does all the talking for him and my pussy talks to Mr. Good Dick too."

Maria's eyes rolled back in her head. She sat still for a moment letting the memories flood her brain.

"Damn, I want to call him right now, shaaaaat."

"It's like that?"

"It's like that. Dr. T is so powerful, he makes me a better person and unbelievably makes my husband a better man."

Natalie shook her head in disbelief.

"Ok, for real now, be serious. Do you think he will be able to help me because I don't how much longer I can continue to feel unwanted by the world? My weight keeps me from so much happiness and I know it will keep me from this Dr. T nigga you talking about. I just have to face it that niggas don't want a big bitch like me."

" Why you gotta be so down on yourself? Girl, that right there ain't sexy. I'm telling you, just call him."

"Fine. I'll call Dr. T and waste my time and get hurt again. I got a lot of shit to offer a nigga, but they can't see it because of how big I am. Honestly Maria, I'm just tired, tired of trying, tired of looking for love, waiting for love, tired of loving love. I'm one more disappointment away from hating love, hating everything about love, hating the thought of love and hating the feeling of love."

Tears fell from Maria's eyes.

"Nat, you have to call him, trust me. He will help you and heal your broken heart. He truly knows what a woman's worth. Black, white, fat, skinny, it doesn't matter. It's almost like his only purpose is to make women happy. He believes in love and wants every woman to be in love with themselves and others. Dr. T really wants us to be in love and not only experience it. I would be divorced and on to the next thing if it wasn't for Dr. T. He made me love me and somehow made my husband love me more and he don't know anything about Dr. T. I think he makes us feel like we're really a lady and once we feel like a lady, nothing else matters."

"Ok Maria, I'll call but I'm a little scared about calling him. What if he says, sorry bitch I can't help you!" Both ladies laughed uncontrollably.

"Girl you crazy, you won't have to worry about that, just call him."

"Ok, I will."

"That's my girl. I'll call you in a couple days just to see how everything went and to say I told you so."

The ladies hug each other and say their goodbyes. After walking away, Maria screamed out to Natalie.

"You better call him!" Natalie laughed.

Chapter 3

I was knocked out sleep, but the R. Kelly ringtone decided that it wanted to go off at about three in the morning, but I answer it anyway.

"Yea this is Dr. T," I stated, mumbling into the handset half asleep. There was no response on the other end.

"Hello? This is Dr. T. Is anyone there?"

"Hi Dr. T, this is Natalie. I got your number from Maria. I'm sorry I'm calling so late. I wasn't sure if I could gather up the nerve to call you or even if you can help me."

"No need to apologize. Just do me one favor Babygirl." She sounded nervous. I felt a need to calm her fears and reassure her I was here for her.

"What's that Dr. T?" Natalie asked, expectation dripping from her tone.

I could tell my voice gave her a sense of comfort from the change in tone. She was already sucked into giving me what I wanted.

"Relax. Maria was right. I'm here for you, anytime of day or night. You need only say the word and my door is open to you, on one condition."

"What's that?"

Good girl. I like the way she followed directions. This made it easier to do my job. Natalie was a little different from Maria. She was a straight shooter, right to the point.

"Look Dr. T, I'm not built like a fashion model, and I'm not so secure with my body. I've been hurt before because of it. Right now...Tonight....I just wanna....."

She cried into the phone, no longer able to speak. It was time for my job to begin.

"You just want to be loved." I said interrupting her.

"How did you know what I was going to say?"

"Who did you ask for when you called me?"

"Dr. T, but what does that have to do with anything? Are you a physic or just some guy who gets off on jerking around women like me?"

"I'm neither. I'm something you've never had. I love women. I love you. I have a gift I'd rather share than keep to myself. My gift is the intimate knowledge of women's deepest needs."

"Is this a game? Are you toying with my emotions? That's what the rest of them did. They played with my feelings and left this broken shattered thing behind."

"Let me put the pieces back together. Let me give you this love rescue."

"Look....Dr. T, I need a love rescue, as you put it, badly, and if it's ok with you..."

"Yes...it's ok with me. Come over, tonight, now. Get up, get dressed, and get here."

"I....but..."

She tried to protest, but I interrupted.

"Come over now. Get a pen and take down these directions." I gave her the directions and quickly went to set the mood for her love rescue.

I lit some incense. The scent of black love filled the house with its sweet smote. I laid a trail of red rose pedals from the living room door to the bed in my room. Scented oil lamps threw soft light on my loving areas in the bedroom and living room.

I lit the last strawberry love scented candle when she arrived. I answered the door.

"Hi, I'm Jason." She looked confused. I felt bad for my lie.

"Do I have the wrong door?"

The wounded expression on her face reminded me this was a woman in pain. I wanted to break the ice, so I put my joke to rest with a smile.

"Come on in, it's me...Dr. T."

She smiled just the way I hoped she would. I apologized. The ice was broken.

"Natalie, baby, you don't have to say anything or do anything. Tonight is all about you."

"I'm very nervous Dr. T. I don't....I don't really know what I'm doing here...with you."

I took off her coat and hung it in my closet, then motioned for her to sit down on the loveseat. I start taking off her shoes, and caressed her feet, without saying a word.

"Dr. T..."

"How was your day baby?"

"What?"

"How was your day?" Her eyes got big, snatching her feet from my hand as if burned.

"My day was bad, really bad." Natalie looked down at her hands clasped in her lap. Her thighs trembled.

"Is there anything you need?" I knew she wanted me to touch her, to need her. I felt her thoughts with knowledge more powerful than love. Being needed and wanted was like a high.

"No, I'm fine," she said trying to play off the depths of her arousal.

Reaching for her hand, then pulling her up from the seat, I took off her clothes one by one. Natalie and I walked into the loving area near the couch. She bit her lip. Tears fell from her eyes.

"I'm afraid Dr. T. I'm so ashamed of how I let myself go all these years. I know it must be hard for you to pretend you could even be aroused by me."

I grabbed her hand, stroked it up against Daddy Dick and let her feel how hard he was.

"Am I hard enough?" I asked. She grabbed me, pulling and tugging on my dick.

Her breath came in short gasps. Her milk chocolate skin was warm to the touch. She was soft, like satin. Her nipples erected from the cold air.

She was sexy. If only she could see it. She had the most beautiful hazel eyes I'd ever seen, almost like butterscotch. She had a style about her that sent vibes all up and through Daddy dick. He throbbed up and down in my Joe boxers.

That luscious body of hers made my mouth water. Natalie was a brick house, proportioned to perfection. She was blessed with large full breasts, rounded hips, thick thighs and a lovely waist.

Natalie stood still. I circled around her thonged ass then lifted the long silky hair off her neck. I slowly began sucking on her sweet flesh like a man starved for chocolate. Natalie moaned with pleasure.

She wasn't getting fucked tonight. She could get that anywhere, for free. Women came to me because they wanted to be loved and treated like a woman should be, with respect and admiration for the female form in general. That's what Dr. T does.

I took Natalie's hand and led her to the bedroom. She looked down at the rose petals, her face radiant and glowing. With my arms wrapped around her, I felt the clench of her thighs against my leg. On the bedside table was peaches and caramel.

I laid Natalie across the rose pedal filled bed and slowly removed her Victoria Secrets with my mouth.

"I wanna feel good, make me feel good!"

Fully undressed now, I kissed and tasted every single spot on Natalie.

"Oooooohhhh shiiiiiit Dr. T!" she cried out.

Natalie would find out more about pleasure tonight. Her moans and groans sound like cries of "it's about timeness."

I went for the caramel and peaches then rolled her over on her stomach. I spread out the peaches from shoulder to shoulder then straight down the center of her back making a "T."

Next I added some caramel for extra flavoring. I sucked, licked and tasted every single spot from her calves to her neck while she struggled not to slide off the bed.

"Ohhh Dooooccccc......Dooooccccc......Dr. T, shiiit!"

That was my cue to flip Natalie over and send my tongue into a whirl wind over her nipples. Her body went crazy, as if she were having a love seizure. Round and round I continued to taste test her nipples. Slowly going up, I kissed her neck and tasted a spot under her chin, then finally reached her full soup cooler lips. I kissed Natalie in only a way that her dream would dream of being kissed.

I tasted the tears Natalie shed while Daddy dick asked her if she was ready. Natalie panted out, "YEEEEEESSSSSSSS."

My tongue overruled Daddy dick this time as I went down to explore places she forgot even existed. My tongue reached Natalie pussy lips. She clenched. I tasted the overflow of Natalie's intoxicating juices and I quickly became F.U.I., "Fucking Under the Influence." I held her thighs tight as if to say you're not going anywhere.

Natalie screamed, "DAMN!...Is your tongue going deep sea diving!" Screams continued to follow.

I came up for air and kissed the inside of Natalie's belly button.

"Can I taste Daddy Dick Dr. T? I wanna taste that chocolate bar."

She doesn't know I have become numb to that question. It does nothing for me. I ignored Natalie's request, but, Daddy Dick must have said something to her because she cried out with words I couldn't understand.

"Can I have Daddy Dick Dr. T, please, I'll be a good girl?" she moaned.

It's time for her to have Daddy Dick. I wanted to take every hurt away from Natalie, I wanted this moment, this instant, my Daddy Dick to make her forget about everything and have her feel like the queen she is.

A loud sigh slash moan came from Natalie when she felt me move inside her body. I moved in and out slowly, not at all in a hurry, she put her thumb in her mouth like a just fed baby. The deeper I went the more she arched her back.

Suddenly Natalie moaned, "I'm a queen, I am a fucking queen, fuckem girl' fuckem."

I laughed to myself. Daddy Dick was talking to her ass.

"Dr. T how in the…oh my. Shit!" Natalie screamed.

"Dr. T, here I cuuuuuum, here I cuuuuuum. Fuuuckkk....shaaattt!"

I knocked it out the park with a hard thrust from Daddy Dick. Just like that Natalie was a new woman. Her head held high and eyes wide open with the, *you know you want me nigga,* look in her eye.

I dressed her back up myself, I said, "Before you ask, that's why I'm Dr. T and yes Daddy Dick was talking to you."

An embarrassed, *but fuck it,* look came over Natalie's face. Putting her earrings back in with my mouth, I whispered, "How do you feel?"

"Like a muthafuckn queen, shit."

"Well babygirl, you have my number, feel free to use it anytime you need to."

"I will.."

I stroked her cheek and gave her a kiss that made her thighs clench together one last time.

Natalie held my hand and said, "Thanks again Dr. T for Daddy Dick."

Chapter 4

On my way from my morning workout, as if last night wasn't enough. I begin to think about all the questions clients have for me that I never answer.

"What makes him happy and who will make Dr. T settle down."

Not really knowing the truth to any of those, I sought answers. So it's time for Dr. T to get in relax mode and figure this thing out. I pull up to my driveway and park my red Lincoln Mark truck.

Strutting inside my house with a walk my clients say screams confidence and a swagger all my own. I toss the keys over near the empty wine bottles Natalie and I had finished off. Then it was off to the shower with an exhausted walk.

I became real good friends with this hot ass water that's massaging my mind and as it worked overtime, I started thinking about the basics, the things that made me tick. I love the ladies. I loved showing a woman she is truly a lady. If I have the slightest clue she doesn't believe she's a queen, I believe it's up to me to put that belief in her. What I can't understand is why I care when it's obvious no one seriously cares about my needs and wants.

Sure I got asked the questions, but that's about it. They never go deeper than the questions. I'm not even sure how I'll act when that person comes and genuinely wants to find out about Terry. I laugh to myself. Shit...I'll be in love then. But my persona, Dr.

T, isn't who I am. Dr. T is a man of many faces. I'm whatever my clients need me to be.

With Maria, I have to be strict and stern with the attitude of, *"this is what I say happens and here is what you gon' do about what I say happens,"* and that works perfect for Maria because she makes a lot of money and she controls everything that's going on in her life that she needs to be taken control of.

The truth of the matter is all of my clients believe I care about their needs and wants more than my own and there's some truth to that.

I reflected in the hot shower that was massaging each part of my body, with each and every drop and sound, smell, and taste like nothing that's ever been thought of.

This shit just felt so damn good, but back to my thought. I really believe deep down, I need these women more than they need me. I need to touch them, I need to listen to them, I need to want them, I need for them to want me and I have become damn good and giving them what they desire only to get what I need. So why do I feel so empty?

I can't help but wonder what it will take for me to get that love that I'm able to give but not receive. Shit....I don't know, but I have to figure this out.

All my clients know about me is I'm Dr. T and I know what they want without them telling me, but really, they know more about Daddy Dick than they do me.

They don't know I'm Terry Davis, a quiet poet and a hopeless romantic. I enjoy, or should I say, I would enjoy spending nights on the beach hearing the soothing sounds of the waves and watching the billions of stars that shine almost as much of the sparkle and shine my lady would have in her eyes.

They don't know I want to experience the times watching my love when she has no idea my eyes, body and soul is locked into hers.
If given the chance to ever love again, she would know and have no doubts about my love for her. She will receive what none of my clients have been able to get, my heart.

The way I'm smiling right now, you would think I'm looking dead at the love of my life. She has long silky black hair and caramel skin that's soft to the touch. Touching her is like an angel sitting on a cloud.

Her eyes are a colored deep dark brown, with a relaxing and inviting gaze that pulls me in closer with each blink. Her lips are soft and full only wanting me to kiss them and stroke them with my own lips. I would be so in tune with her mind that it's almost like I see her mind and I can touch it.

She would be shy and soft spoken, but strong, independent and a true lady that knows how to make a man feel like a man. Shit, almost like a female Dr. T. But what I would love the most about her is her need and want to love someone the way she is in love with love itself. Damn! Again like another female Dr. T.

To say I'm not in love would be wrong, I'm in love with love, but love right now seems not to love me back. So for now, I'm content with making every woman be in love and have it love them back.

An hour after reflecting in the shower, it was time to get out and dry off, but I refused the help drying towel for now.

Naked, I walked into my room with my dick swinging and hanging freely, reminding me of the time Maria was here and I was walking around bare ass'd. I would come running upstairs with my dick swinging and bumping from thigh to thigh and I would catch her biting her lip gazing at my manhood.

Laughing out loud at that memory, I pick out the suit I'll wear to go get me some lunch. It was instilled in me to always look my best wherever I am.

With the sun breaking through my window and the sun drying off the water that sliding down off my chest to my six pack, I lay my black suit with pin stripes across the bed and run my naked ass in the bathroom to go ahead and grab some assistance from the drying towel to dry me off.

After I dry off and brush my clean cut hair, I start trimming my goatee so I can feel like I look. Sharp. After I put on my cologne and put the finishing touches on my suit, it was time to head out. So I grabbed the keys to my BMW 745 and went on my way to what I had the feeling of it being an adventurous day.

Chapter 5

"Aww shiiit, you got that look on your face." Maria said while taking a seat.

Grinning sarcastically, Natalie says, "Girl, what you talking about?"

"You know damn well you know what I'm talking about. That's that '*I just had Daddy Dick*' look. Trust me, I know that look and shit I'm bout due for that look myself. Now stop trippin and tell me everything that happened."

"It ain't nothing to........."

Maria interrupts, "Come on Nat, you know you wanna tell somebody so you might as well tell me."

With a long pause, Natalie says, "Ok, well I called later that night and.......hold on girl, somebody calling me."

"Hello, this is Natalie."

"Hey Natalie, this is Dr. T, I was calling you to make sure your day is going good for you and to let you know to keep that beautiful smile on your face."

"Dr. T, I wasn't expecting your call and I was just thinking about you."

"Well Babygirl, if you need anything just give me a call. Oh yea, tell Maria Dr. T says hey."

"How did you know I'm with Maria?"

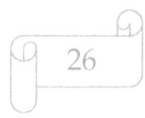

"Come on Natalie, I'm Dr. T, I'll talk to you later."

"Ok, bye Dr. T." She sat there still amazed.

"That man is amazing. Oh yea, Dr. T wanted me to tell you hey."

"So girl, tell me what happened."

"Well I called him later that night and we talked on the phone for a while and without me even telling him, this nigga gave me directions to his house. I like his confidence in himself that he just knew I would come."

"So did you go?" Maria asked already knowing the answer.

"Shit yea I went. I had to see for myself about this
Dr. T nigga. Oh....girl, this nigga broke the ice good by playing a nice lil' joke on me when I arrived."

In shock, Maria says, "Dr. T jokes? He never jokes with me; it always seems like a business meeting with him......a damn good business meeting though."

"Come on Maria, you said yourself Dr. T knows what we want without us telling him. He knew for me to be relaxed he had to make me laugh. Anyway, he knew just what to say, just what to do. Before I get into the good stuff, let me ask you...uhhhhh, did his dick talk to you?"

Pausing with her eyes closed as if Maria is listening to Daddy Dick now, she says, "Girl, Daddy Dick is talking to me right now."

"Ok, well now I know I ain't trippin then. But girl, for the first time, I didn't have to think about my weight, I didn't have to tell myself I wasn't sexy. For the first time in a long time, I actually felt like a lady. Dr. T touched me where I wanted to be touched, he kissed every spot I felt insecure about and he said all the right things. How does this nigga do this shit?"

Sipping on her Appletini, Maria says, "Nat, all I can say is what he tells me and that is. Don't question things that can't be explained. But I still have questions ya know. Like, why does he do this and how does he do it. So many times, I just want to please him and love him, but love him only as a thank you for what he does, and I think he knows that, that's why he won't let me please him."

Gulping down her long island ice tea, Natalie says, "Shit, I know. I damn near begged him to let me suck that big, wide ass Daddy Dick, and he ignored me, but it's cool cuz, shaaaat, he did some things to me I didn't even know was possible."

"But it's like you said Maria, I only wanted to please him as a thank you for what he was doing to me. Is it just a, *onetime* thing with Dr. T, or can I go back for more?"

Laughing out loud then saying in a secretive voice, Maria responded.

"Nat, I been going back for almost 2 years now and it doesn't always have to be about sex, he knows when you want love, sex or just to talk."

"I wish he can somehow make me lose some weight so I can find my soul mate."

Looking down and then back up, Maria says, "Nat, Dr. T may not be dropping the weight off of you, but he is doing something even better for you."

"Shit, and what's that?"

"Well, besides giving you Daddy Dick."

Interrupting, Natalie says, "Yea, he's definitely doing that."

"Seriously Nat, he's giving you confidence and that's important to have, especially when you don't have it."

"Wait, hold up Maria. Are you trying to say you don't have confidence? Shit girl, look at you. You make a hell of a lot of money and I'll kill to have the body you got. Girl, how in the hell you lacking confidence? You're married so you always have somebody to go home to every night. I love me some Daddy Dick, but I can't go home to that every night!"

"Waiter, can I have another apple martini, and make it stronger this time?" begged Maria.

"Damn girl, you ok......Hello.....Maria?"

"Nat, I need to talk to you about something and it's kinda hard to talk about."

"Awww shit, something juicy!"

"Come on Nat, its serious."

"Ok girl. What's wrong?"

Maria took a long sip of her drink and took a deep breath once she swallowed.

"I'm not as happy as you think. The only time I'm really happy is when I'm with Dr. T."

"What about when you're with your husband?"

"Girl, me and Juan divorced about a year ago."

"What the hell, are you serious? Why the fuck you just now telling me this shit Maria, I thought we were friends?"

"I was embarrassed Nat."

"Oh, you was embarrassed, kinda how I am about my weight?"

"Hold on Nat, my phone is ringing, hold on. Hello?"

"Hey Maria, this Dr. T. I felt I needed to check on you. Do you need to talk or something?"

"Uhhmmm, naw Dr. T, I'm ok."

Blurting out in anger, Natalie says "Does Dr. T know?"

"Shhhhhh Natalie!"

"Do I know what?"

"Nothing Dr. T, I'm ok."

"Maria....who am I?"

" You're Dr. T, why?"

"Well, you know I know something is wrong, so I'll let you finish talking to Natalie, and then you bring your sexy ass over to the house later ok babe?"

Maria sobered up for a quick second and couldn't stop herself from blushing.

"Ok Dr. T, I'll be there, bye."

"Ok girl, back to my question. Does Dr. T know that you're divorced?"

"Why does he need to know? Everything is fine the way it is."

"No it's not Maria and I'll tell you why everything is not fine."

"Why?"

With a, *'I know something you don't know'* laugh, Natalie said.

"Because you're in love with Dr. T."

"Nat, how can I be in love with Dr. T when I gave you his number so you can get you some and help you out?"

"Because you can't or don't want to accept the fact you're in love with a man that can't love you back."

Maria finished off her Apple Martini and started packing her things together.

"You know what. I don't need this right now, so I'm going to leave and get ready for a night with the man I'm supposedly in love with."

"Maria? Wait. Do you want me to stop talking to Dr. T?"

Maria shouldered her Coach purse and put on matching sunglasses.

"No because he's not my man." Maria said and walked away.

Chapter 6

"Hey Beautiful, How are you doing today?"

"Welcome to Shania's, and my day is like shit." Brittany, the drama filled waitress said.

"Awww baby, don't ever let someone still your joy, you hear me? Now put that sexy smile back on your face." Instantly, Brittany started blushing and grabbed a menu.

"There you go babe, walk that walk. Twist it, miss it, kiss it and diss it."

"Dr. T, what does that even mean?" Brittany asked with her hand on her hip and that laugh I like.

"Hell if I know gorgeous, but it got you to smile didn't it?"

"Anyway Dr. T, your friend Jordan is here, do you wanna go sit with him?"

"Yea, JB is here, yea I'll go sit with his crazy ass."

Jordan Billings is my crazy best friend, but he's cool though. He's an architect and already married with kids. He wants to be in my shoes so bad. It's amazing how people sometimes admire where you are in your life when you never wanted this for yourself, but instead, you want what they have and they have no clue whatsoever.

"Look at this Dr. T nigga here. What's up Dr. T, you save any lives today?"

"What's going on JB, still crazy I see?"

"Damn nigga, you going to a funeral or something? Why the hell you always got on a suit and don't say it's to impress the ladies. You know these girls would want you if you looked like shit with mustard spread over it."

"Naw man, I just like to look good and ain't nothing wrong with that."

"So what's going on with you today, who you going to see today, probably Maria again?" JB said with the, '*whatever nigga*' look.

"What you trying to say JB?"

"Nothing, it just seems you always with Maria now. Any newbies besides that fat one you somehow fucked?"

"Come on JB, Natalie is cool; there's no need to be talking about her like that."

Jordan is cool, but we do have different minds and different philosophies. He thinks all heavyset people should be with heavyset people if they aren't single that is. He's only interested in the model type, which there's nothing wrong with that, but me myself, if she's a lady and, I feel she doesn't feel like a lady, then Dr. T has to be Dr. T and make any and all women feel like queens.

"Naw, no newbies right now, but I'm not always with Maria."

"Whatever nigga, you and Maria need to gon' stop trippin and hook up as a couple. I don't see why you won't. Nigga I'll break that Latino's back in every night. Gon' put your seed in that man."

"First off, Maria's married. Secondly, I don't want Maria like that, if I did, I would give in to her desires to suck this Daddy Dick!"

"What the fuck, you won't let her suck yo' shit?" JB screamed as he put his drink down.

"Naw, man, it's a way of keeping it just the way I want it and plus I know they only want to do it as a thank you for what I'm doing to them."

"Who you about to call, Maria?" JB asked as he saw me whipping out my phone.

Taking a sip of my strawberry lemonade drink, I ignoreed JB and called Natalie.

"Hello? This is Natalie."

"Hey Natalie, this is Dr. T, I was calling you to make sure your day is going good for you and to let you know to keep that beautiful smile on your face."

"Dr. T, I wasn't expecting call! I was just thinking about you!"

"Well babygirl, if you need anything just give me a call. Oh yea, tell Maria, Dr. T says hey."

"How did you know I'm with Maria?"

"Come on Natalie, I'm Dr. T, I'll talk to you later."

"Ok, bye Dr. T."

Laughing out loud, Jordan says, "Terry, you are one smooth ass nigga, do you mind if I call my wife and do what you just did to Natalie?"

Knowing Jordan was just joking, but I respond, "Not at all JB, it may get you some ass that you haven't been getting."

That shut Jordan up real quick!

"Anyway JB, how's work and the family going, ya know, besides not getting any ass?"

"Whateva Terry. Everything is going good, the kids and the misses are fine. What about you Terry? Seriously man, when are you going to settle down with somebody and start having some kids? You are almost 30 years old and it's about that time. Plus, I can tell when something is bothering you. On the cool my nigga, what's going on?" JB asked while leaning forward.

Little does Jordan know, I get these types of questions all the time from Maria and Natalie. I had time to think about this same shit when I was in the shower. I don't need to be talking or thinking about this right now. I debated whether or not to give JB the same answer I gave them or, would I just ignore him. In the middle of my thoughts, Brittany twists her sexy ass over to the table and sit next to me.

"Dr. T, would you like any......."

Before she could finish, I take the back of my hand and stroke her cheeks. Instantly I see goose bumps on top of goose bumps on her shoulders. I lean over and whisper in her ear.

" Baby you come over here asking if I need anything when I know exactly what you want."

"Oh you do, huh? How is that?" She asked softly, already giving in to me like a victim being hypnotized by the sensual tone in my whisper.

"Who am I?"

She moved her head as if she already felt me penetrating inside her. Her eyes were closed and her mouth opened.

" Who am I?" I repeated in a soft, slow deeper voice.

"Dr. T, you are Dr. T baby."

"There you go love."

"Dr. T, uuummm I was wondering if you, uuuhhhh."

"Of course I will sexy. I'll see you in an hour."

"Ok Dr. T, see you then, I can't wait."

I watched Brittany as she walked away and it was the perfect walk and she possessed the perfect body. I just loved to watch her sashay away, but Brittany was all about Brittany.

"What the fuck, how in the hell? Terry you are too smooth for your own good!"

"That's not it JB, I just gotta give them what I know they want to make them feel like a queen."

"But that chick didn't even tell you what she wanted. How did you know?"

"JB, what did she call me?"

" Dr. T, but how did..."

"JB, I'll tell you like I tell them, don't question what can't be explained."

"Ok, at least tell me what she wanted?" I measured him up to see if he could really handle it.

"Man, she wanted to know if I can meet her in the break room on her lunch break."

"You are one lucky man. Damn you one fucking lucky man. Seriously though man, answer my question. I only ask because you my boy and I can tell when something ain't right with you. You been in a lil' snappy mood lately, especially when I get to talking about how good things are with wifey and the kids, so tell me what's going on? Tell me what do you want, what do you dream about man, fa real?"

"Dreams are cheap JB, it's the details that made me. I use to dream. I use to dream of one day having what you have, a beautiful wife, and beautiful kids and then I came across one woman who just did me wrong and basically made me feel like it was my entire fault."

Not once did I look at JB while I was talking. I sat there drinking my lemonade and looking inside it as if all my answers were at the bottom of the glass.

"Man, you never really told me in detail what happened. You say the details made you, well what details turned you into this smooth ass, yet stupid ass Dr. T, if your ass want a family? It's not as hard as you making the shit out to be Terry," JB said, in a duh nigga kind of way.

I wallowed in what seemed like forever solitude, holding my glass of hidden answers. All the memories were coming back and I could remember it like it was yesterday and instantly, I was taken back.

"Hey baby, how was your day?" I said as I gave my girlfriend Renee of three years, a kiss on the cheek.

Renee was everything I ever wanted in a woman. She was beautiful, smart, and intelligent and what every man wanted; a lady in the streets and a fucking freak in the bedroom.

She possessed all the qualities that you would want in a wife and mother. She was very thoughtful, caring and nurturing and strong when she needed to be.

Physically, the Lord blessed her with something special. Renee stood 5'8" tall and has nice dark mahogany skin that I loved to taste every inch of. She had medium to long hair that was wavy and just long enough for me to pull when I would have her bent over. She had the most perfect lips, made just for wrapping them around my dick. I got chills and a hard on just thinking about them.

Her eyes were a hazel brown, and her skin was as soft as air. When she smiled, she had the most perfect dimples that God could have ever designed. She was my world and I was sure I was at the point of making her mine forever.

You see, earlier that day I left early to go to work, but instead I went a purchased a gift for my beautiful Renee and couldn't wait to give it to her.

I was finally home and I had something set up very special for her and couldn't wait until it was over because it's all I've been able to think about all day. I was eager to put my briefcase down and go love on my baby.

"Baby you doing ok? How was your day?" I asked as I made me a nice drink.

"It was ok." Renee said, quick and to the point.

"Baby you ok?" I asked, knowing she wasn't by her tone.

"I'm cool….Actually, Terry we need to talk and it can't wait any longer." Renee said as she kept her legs crossed and turned back to look at me signaling for me to come to where she was.

She shook her foot nervously and panicky. Her eyes, that I once thought was beautiful, seemed so hurt and full of sorrow and pain. Her arms were folded and slowly tears started falling from her eyes.

"Baby what's wrong?" I asked as I quickly went to console her.

"You….this…this bullshit life is what's wrong." She said as she threw her arms out.

Mind you, she stays with me in my 4,000 square foot home and three classic cars in the driveway, and also, Renee does not have to worry about money, she does not work, and I pay all the bills. I dick her down at least twice a day, every day, so hearing the term bullshit life definitely struck a chord with me.

"Bullshit life huh, explain?" I asked as I took a gulp of my previously sipped Brandy.

"Well Terry….you just…there's no way you can….I mean, you just don't make me happy…and….and you just….."

It always amazes me when someone has to tell you something bad, 'you' gets used a lot more. Renee went on to name all the things I don't do and I just continued to drink my Brandy while she said all she had to say, which involved a lot of 'you's.'

"And another thing, Terry, you just don't satisfy me the way I want to be satisfied. You are a horrible lover. You don't listen to me. You don't pay me any attention. You don't fucking notice me any goddamn more Terry. I'm supposed to be your girlfriend and you never pay me any fucking attention, all you talk about is your writing, real estate and going to play ball. I get sick of hearing about that shit!" Renee continues to vent.

Meanwhile, I have made my way back to the kitchen to make me another drink because somehow, my glass of Brandy suddenly was empty.

When I came back into the living area, Renee was still talking and I heard every word she said. I not only heard, but I listened to every word she said.

"Bottom line Terry, I'm just not happy with you anymore and I want to break up, now!"

Again, I looked in the bottom of my glass for answers, and all I found was some damn good Brandy.

"So, I don't listen to you huh? Ok, ask me anything about what you think I wasn't listening about, go ahead?" I said, still looking in my glass.

"Ok, Terry, there's a list of things I can ask you."
"Go for it!"

"The other day when I was telling you about my best friend..." Quickly, I interrupted.

"Do you mean when you told me about your best friend Denise and how her husband cheated on her, but Denise couldn't find any evidence, so she planned to set him up by saying she will be home late?"

"Instead she hid in the yard to spy on him? Yes, Renee I remember that whole conversation. I also remember thinking how beautiful you looked in the new ear rings you bought. That was a new outfit too right? But go ahead to the next thing."

"Fine Terry, what about the time when I was telling you that I don't know what to do anymore, when I was telling you I feel useless since I don't work?"

"Ok, you mean that conversation when I gave you plenty of suggestions of things you could do to make yourself not feel so helpless, I even offered to pay for you to go to law school since you said that was your dream, to be a lawyer. Next?" I said while leaning back and stretching out on my leather recliner.

"Well, you don't fuck me or make love to me the way I want to anymore and I just can't take this shit anymore!"

"Ok, fuck you or make love to you like what, like this."

Her eyes were closed as she felt me enter inside her while making both of her knees buckle simultaneously.

Renee's eyes squinted as she felt me touch her with the tips of my fingers and I breathed erotic breaths into her ear that left her gasping and panting. Renee reacted by melting in my hand and tossing out orgasmic moans.

She finally opened her eyes and realized, I never physically touched her yet, in fact, all I said was baby I love you. Just like that, she was given a mental orgasm. I got up from my recliner and walked over to Renee. First I kissed her tears away and loved how they tasted on my lips.

Next, I proceeded to taste every inch of Renee and I knew she couldn't resist it because I damn near felt juices explode on my fingers like a waterfall when I moved them inside her.

Renee was undressed and off into another world as I palmed her ample breast and circled her nipples with my tongue while slightly blowing, that alone made four letter curse words escape her breath.

Through the rhythm of her *mmm's* and the blues in her *ahh's*, my hands indented themselves onto her thighs.

My nature parted through remnants of her soul and into her heavens and earths, while love colored moans escaped her breath.

Passion tears hung from her eyelids and the juices from planet Renee made for one hell of an adult beverage that I couldn't pass up. I drank from her well and became intoxicated instantly, and instantly I was sobered.

I was sure that when I experienced the sweetness of her exuberant moistened garden while she experienced the stiffness of my renaissance manhood, we would fall in love over and over again. One hand was pushing me away while the other hand and her legs pulled me back in. She was panting out moans and gasping for runaway air.

Renee's pussy knew my tongue very well and as soon as my tongue moved down her sweet garden, she instantly started quivering. My tongue deep sea dove inside her oceans of pleasantry and I enjoyed the sweet creamy decadence of her moistened offerings. Renee screamed and moaned in what seemed like so many different languages I spelled out *'how bilingual'* with my tongue inside her essence.

After few more juicy eruptions from Renee's garden of sensationalism, I arrived drenched and covered in her sweet amazing grace. On top of Renee, I entered her and always enjoy what I have deemed 'the sigh.' It was time, I watched her eyes close again, and I wanted Renee to roll her eyes back to me as she feels me penetrate.

I wanted her to feel my nature grow and part through her gardens of love and rain on my nature and in turn, I'll water her garden, while planting my seed.

I entered and kept entering and Renee passionately beat on my shoulders with her fist moaning out "fuck" her eyes closed tightly in ecstasy and teardrops streamed from her eyes, which I kissed away.

I ran my fingers through her tangled hair and whispered in her ear

"Cum for me baby."

I always enjoyed when she followed directions. Renee was soaking wet and screaming out more four letter curse words as I felt her waterfall on my nature. Planting her legs over my shoulders, I penetrated deeper and deeper until she let out an *'it's in my stomach cough.'* Renee screamed and cried into ecstasy which was only motivation for me.

Thoughts of *'yea bitch, you said I don't fuck you right or make love to right, but yet yo' ass already came 3 times and I ain't even started,'* fluttered through my mind.

I threw Renee in plenty more positions and she must have had something to talk to God about very important because she kept calling out to Him.

I exploded inside her while in the doggy style position and as I continued to thrust. Renee was reminded of the power of my dick because as I exited her numb entry way, she stayed there still moaning, still groaning, still bent over. She was also was reminded of the power of my dick when she turned over and her legs laid there throbbing, but throbbing in pure enjoyment.

Renee tried to get up to walk around but failed at her many attempts.

"I was in love with your heart I thrust slowly but surely and each time, I fell in love with you all over again because I was just that close to physically feeling your heart. I was in love with your heart babygirl and I was in love with knowing you were my world and I thrust physically into your essence and mentally into your emotional presence. I fell in love with the journey we were about to start. I was in love with you and I was close to mentally tasting your heart, but now, all I can say is sorry I can't fuck you or make love to you the way you want." I said, pillowtalk like towards Renee. I then apologized for not fucking her the way she wanted and got up. That was the last of Renee.

"So what the hell happened to the surprise you had for her, shit nigga what was the surprise?" JB wondered in suspense.

It was funny and I felt bad about reliving that part of my life, but I felt good because JB was so drawn into the story.

"The surprise JB was an engagement ring." I said signaling for some more lemonade.

"Why didn't you ever tell me all this before man? All you told me was there was no more Renee. You never went into details."

"JB, it is what it is. Details are nothing more than what they are; details that made me."

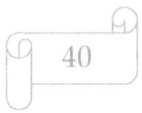

"Well did you ever find out the real reason she broke up with you?" I let out a sarcastic laugh.

"Yep, I ran into her a couple years later and she finally told me."

"Well nigga, don't keep a brutha waiting."

"Apparently, she met a big time basketball player that just signed a big contract and she met him the same day I bought her the ring. He was crazy about her and she obviously liked her chances with him, so shit, she made up some bogus shit about me not doing this, not doing that. The funny things is JB, for a long time, I actually believed it was my fault."

"Damn nigga, that's fucked up. Was she at least still with the dude?" Again, a sarcastic laugh escaped my mouth.

"Nope."

"Damn, so you were gonna ask her to marry you? Oh well, man her loss, she could have had a good guy and been married by now, but she let some ball player fuck that up." JB said in hopes of trying to comfort me, but he's about to be in more shock.

"Yea man, we could have been married by now and with a kid because after I dicked her down, she ended up getting pregnant with my baby, but decided to get an abortion because the ball player told her he wouldn't be with her if she had my baby." I sat there gazing off into something nonexistent and JB sat there with his mouth basically touching the floor.

"Man, don't even worry about that. You muthafuckin Dr. T now, fucking all these beautiful women. Yea it's fucked up what Renee did, but trust me Terry, you living every man's dream right now, fucking all these beautiful females man." I stared, just shy of evil at JB.

"JB, honestly fuck a dream. I told you dreams are cheap, details are what made me and what will continue to make me.

Everything Renee has done to me has made me what I am. I am a man that has come to love seeing a woman happy and in love because I was accused of not doing this to the woman I loved. Before I knew the truth, I felt so bad and believed everything Renee told me. I told myself that no woman would ever cross my path and not believe she's a queen and not believe she's loved. You say I'm living the dream and I say fuck a dream, dreams are cheap, details are what made me."

Again we share the same thoughts about each other life without him even knowing it. With a wife and kids, I considered him to be the lucky one.

I said fuck it to it all and I pulled out my Iphone to make a call. This time I felt I needed to call Maria, something just didn't seem right.

"Hello?"

"Hey Maria, this Dr. T, I felt I needed to check on you. Do you need to talk or something?"

"Uhhmmm, naw Dr. T, I'm ok." I heard Natalie in the background asking Maria if I knew.

"Do I know what?"

"Nothing Dr. T, I'm ok."

"Maria....who am I?"

"You're Dr. T, why?"

"Well, you know I know something is wrong, so I'll let you finish talking to Natalie, and then you bring your sexy ass over to the house later ok babe?"

"Ok Dr. T, I'll be there, bye."

Shaking his head laughing, Jordan yellsed "Nigga, you gon' be tired!"

"Well as long as I make them feel like princesses, I don't care how tired I get."

"Anyway man, I gotta go back to work and finish up on some things. When you not too tired, let's go out and kick it sometime."

Jordan was always trying to get me out to go do something with him. Really he just wanted to get away from the wife and kids for a while.

"Yea, we can do that. Don't forget to call your wife just to see how her day is going and if she needs anything."

"Ok Terry."

"I'm serious JB, that's guaranteed booty right there!"

He laughed and walked away.

Chapter 7

I'm still sitting at the table, just waiting on the signal from fine ass Brittany to motion me to the break room. So I decided to do what I do best, write.

I took out my pen and notepad. First I think to myself, what I could write about…love, sex, or romance. They all tie in together but they are very different. I'll stay on the romantic thing.

So after thinking for a while, I get to writing and while I'm writing, my brain told my eyes to look up at the most beautiful person to ever cross my path. Feeling me gazing at her, she looks at me and smile then goes back doing what she was doing.

Now normally, Dr. T would take over right here, but for some reason I stayed shy and reserved to this beautiful person. She had long silky hair and her skin had me imagining the softest cloud. Her eyes pulled me in and already had me giving all she desired.

The sight of her was powerful, so powerful that I could feel her tingling touch. I snapped myself out of it. As I mentioned earlier, Dr. T would already be over there, but I just couldn't find myself going there. I couldn't see myself just having her as another client and the fact that I'm still sitting here confirms that. I continue to write, but now it's a different subject: '*Out of Love.*'

Out of Love
I believe I have spoken them before, words of
love and words of hate
I gave all of me, all of my love and I put my trust in fate
My love was received, but love wasn't stamped
and delivered back to me
It was merely kept with no importance on how it came
to be
So I sit here and express the sadness of my heart
And try my damnest to imagine me and you
apart
Never, not once have I ran out of Love
But your love have flown away from me like a dove
I'll stay here sulking over the emptiness of my
heart
And believe one this real love thing will begin to
start
But until then, I'll pray that someone give my
confidence a shove
And I will rejoice when the day comes when I no longer
run out of love.

Finally, I built up some confidence and I walked over to her table with what Maria calls '*a cool ass walk Papi.*'

"Hi, is there anyone sitting here with you?"

With the softest most powerful voice, she answered my question and one that I've yet to ask.

"No, would you like to sit there?"

"Yes, this may come off as corny, but I saw you alone and you are so beautiful that I just had to come over and introduce myself and get to know you. By the way, my name is Terry, Terry Davis."

"Hi Terry, yes it was corny. Couldn't you have come up with a better line than that?" she said with a gorgeous smile.

Already I like how this is going, she's testing my confidence and that was sexy to me.

"I could have, but I believe in saying what's on my mind and speaking the truth rather than sitting over there at my table thinking about what I would say to you. Corny or not, you'll get what's meant to come out, not thought about." She sat there staring at me and then looked me up and down as if she was trying to figure me out.

"Is that a line Mr. Davis, and by the way my name is Patrice, Patrice Williams."

"No Ms. Williams that was the truth."

"So Terry, what where you writing over there, some lines you would tell me?"

We both laughed at her known attempts to give me a hard time.

She will soon find out I'm smooth, I'm calm and, I'm like no other man she's ever encountered.

"Actually Patrice, by looking at your notepad, I was doing the same thing you were doing."

Looking down at her notepad she says, "You were writing poetry?"

"Yea, I always come to Shania's and write poetry, it's a relaxing place to write." She looked at me with disbelief in her eyes.
Laughing I say, "Aww, that baby don't believe me?"

"No, I don't. Where is it at?" she asked with that beautiful smile and a twinkle in her eye.

With no hesitation, I let her read my poem. As she read, her eyes jump as if she read something interesting. Her full soup cooler lips perked up as if she agreed with something I wrote. That just gave me time to bask in her beauty.

"So...Terry? Are you really running out of love?"

"I'll just say that, love really is playing hide and seek with me, but something suddenly hinted to me that I'll find it soon."

I didn't give her time to respond to the last comment I made.

"Can I now read what you got Miss Ma'am?"

"Yea, here you go and, uhh we will revisit your last comment. My poem is '*In Our Bed*.' It's something I always seen myself doing to the love of my life. Ok, just read it."

In the silence and stillness of the night
I stare at you with the moon sharing its light
There are no words are being shared
Only the love of each other which God so gracefully
paired
Throughout the night, we sleep in each other's arms
As we admire the feeling of our love that forms
I could only dream about my heart making love
to yours
And watching you enjoy the essence of mine as
it pours
I'll never forget the excited tears my love shed
And the way we caress each other in our bed

"Wow Patrice. Do you know how I told you I tell you what I have to tell you without thinking about it, whether it's corny or not?"

"Yea Terry, why?"

"Well, by reading your poem. You were writing that just for me and I was writing mine just for you."

Looking at me like nigga you crazy, but only if she knew, I was dead serious.

"Terry, you saying I wrote this poem because I saw you over there and I wanted this to be you and you wrote *Out of Love* because you want my love?"

"Naw Patrice, you wrote *In our Bed* because you where envisioning yourself doing that to your husband, right?"

"Yea, so, what does that have to do with you?"

Without saying another word, I reach into my briefcase and pull out another poem.

"Here Patrice, read this and then you will know what I'm talking about."

In Our Bed
All I want is to lie in our bed
And enjoy the time when no words are said
As we spend our days loving our touching
And we spend our nights cherishing our cuddling
I just want to lie in our bed as you lie on my
chest

Knowing that it's forever and we can put our worries to rest
Because as I look into your eyes and you stare back into mine
We will believe the moon as it slices through and sparkles and shine
Knowing that you are the only woman I love
We'll fly off to love land like two beautiful doves
Spending my life with one person was something I dread
But there's no doubt in my mind that I'm in love every time we lie in our bed

"Wow that's definitely weird right there, the same title and everything. That is..." both of us were left in shock. So I decided to just jump in.

"Patrice, just by sitting here talking to you and getting to know you a little bit, I have to say that there is more I want to know about you. Is there any chance, I mean if you're not involved with anyone we can go out one day?" I felt like I was in school again writing a letter to a girl asking if she would go out with me, yes or no, circle one.

"Well Terry, I don't know about going out with you, but here's my number and we can talk about that little comment you made about you finding love soon. You are definitely an interesting person and I'll be lying if I said I didn't want to get to know you too."

Packing up her things, she says I'm looking forward to hearing from you."

"Same here gorgeous"

She walked off and I was left looking at her long silky

hair and Coke bottle figure. With nothing but good thoughts filling my brain about this woman, I couldn't help but think about how I would tell her about this Dr. T thing I got going on.

Speaking of Dr. T, Brittany motioned for me to come to the break room. I couldn't turn her down just because I met somebody I'm interested in, right?

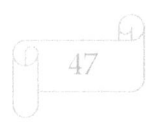

I still have that need, that want to make every lady feel like a lady so I grabbed my briefcase and walked to the break room.

Chapter 8

"Hi Dr. T, come on in baby, I'm ready for ya. You don't need to lock the door, not unless you feel you need to."

Like I said before, Brittany was all about Brittany, which is not necessarily a bad thing. She knows what she wants and she won't waste time getting it.

"Hey gorgeous, I'm not worried about the door. The only thing on my mind right now is you."

"What you plan on doing to me Dr. T?"

"First I'm going to warm you up by singing to that pussy and make your juices sing back to me."

"Good, because I'm bout do for a love rescue, so bring your sexy ass on over here with that one helluva swag you got."

I walked right on over and got face to face with Brittany. I stopped so she could brace herself for what was about to happen to her. I stared into her eyes as if I saw something beyond her hazel pupils. Brittany opened her mouth to begin to speak, before anything came out, I allowed my lips to barely touch hers while I grabbed hold of her body.

Caressing her with my fingertips and with the base of my palm I slowly and meticulously massaged her way into heaven for a while. Tasting a sweet spot behind her ear, I began to send my tongue in circles and then start hearing the *ooohs,* and *aaahhs,* that have now becomeBrittany's first language.

Whispering in her ear, I ask, "How does this feel?"

"Like heaven Dr. T, this feels like heaven. It feels like a hundred hands are touching me. How are you doing this babe?"

Slowly kissing Brittany from the bottom of her chin to the beginning of her neck, I start undressing her, still tasting every piece of what seems like chocolate caramel.

Then I removed her bra with my hands and teeth.

"Aahhhhhhhh, shhiiiitt Dr. T!"

I grabbed hold of her breast, both fitting perfectly into each of my hands. Licking, sucking, tasting her nipples.

Brittany moaned and squirmed with each squeeze of her
breast and suckle of her nipples.

I felt her jump as I kissed with a slight bite on each side of her stomach slowly moving toward her navel and then on down to the inside of her legs and just outside of her wet pussy.

I enjoyed watching her pussy lips smile at me, I showed my appreciation for the smile by introducing my tongue to her pussy.

Brittney was laid out across the break room table.

"Brittany, its lunch time."

I heard a sigh of relief when my tongue penetrated
inside of her and instinctively she arched her back as I
tasted all of her juices.

"Dr........Dr.........Dr......"

"Damn baby, it's Dr. T." is what I wanted to say, but I understood my tongue had Brittany all discombobulated and shit.

I held her thick, track trained legs high in the air as her clit played hide-n-go get it with my tongue and my tongue definitely got it, all of it.

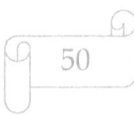

Brittany tried in vain to keep from yelling and screaming. I felt her grabbing her breast while I continued to feast and, while I tasted all she had to offer, I feel and extra pair of hands stroking my back.

Not really giving a damn about the other pair of hands, as long as they came with breast and another pussy, Dr. T was cool.

"Uhhhh baby, you may want to look up?"

"Why baby, that shit is feeling too damn good?"

"Brittany, just look up, we have company."

Dr. T had an audience now. I just wanted to bring this beautiful Asian chick right on in the mix, but it wasn't about me, it was about Brittany right now. So hidden behind my expression was
really me praying that Brittany was ok with it.

"Tren, what are you doing in here?"

"Uhh, Brittany this is the break room and I need a break." Tren said without ever taking her eyes off Daddy
Dick.

"Fuck it" I said, not caring about what they had going on. I saw two women that need the services of Dr. T and his Daddy Dick. I went back down and put the finishing touch on pussy tasting Brittany and slowly pulled Tren to meand started undressing her.

All I could think about right now was that I'll have to break a rule I have just this one time. Somebody will taste Daddy Dick today.

"Dr. T, what you doing, she can't co..."

I went back to tasting Brittany and that killed that noise she was talking. I laid Tren right next to Brittany and I tell her, "Brittany, tell Tren who I am."

"Tren, this is Dr. T."

"Now, Brittany just relax, you know I can make you feel like you the only one in the room and that goes for you too Tren. I see how you staring at this Daddy Dick. He won't hurt you suga."

With Brittany and Tren both laid out on the table as if I was about to perform surgery on them, I took one hand and undressed Tren and with the other hand, I started to feel how warm Brittany really was.

As I felt the inside of Brittany, I went down for my first taste of some Asian pussy. With her thick accent, Tren moaned.

"Dr. T.!"

There you go babe, enjoy what I'm doing. Shit, everybody else does!

With all the juices I tasted today, I shouldn't be thirsty for days, not to mention I still have to see Maria's fine ass tonight.

Tren was spilling out of kinds of juices. My tongue
went deeper and spinned faster and her screams followed. Brittany moaned out, "Be quiet Tren, before someone else comes and take this shit from us."

"Tren?"

"Yes."

"Who am I?" And all I got was moans, ok she'll pay for that.
When I finished feasting on Tren, I ordered Brittany to kiss Tren and being in the moment, Brittany followed my demanding orders. She knew the more she obeyed, the better Daddy Dick would feel.

As I watch Brittany and Tren kiss passionately, I slid around and bent Tren over and went to work. Slowly I allowed Tren to enjoy the entrance of Daddy Dick, and as penetrated, her mouth opened and
she couldn't focus on kissing Brittany. I held her by her thin hips, thrusting deeper and harder now I say, "Tren?"

"Yes?"

"Who am I?"

"Dr........Dr.......Dr.........Dr."

Every time my thighs touched her ass, she said Dr.

Dr.........Dr......Dr........Dr..." I slowed up my stroke just so I could hear her say it right.

"Who am I?"

"Dr. T....Dr. T baby, shiiiit, you are Dr. ......fuuuuuuckkkk!"

Ok, back to regular scheduled stroking. While I'm still inside her, I flip Tren over and put her legs on my shoulders with her still laid out on the table. Brittany came over and started rubbing me all over.

I couldn't neglect her, so I sat her on my shoulders and started feasting again, still giving Tren the business, only now Brittany was holding Tren's legs up.

I continued to feast upon the nectar that was of Brittany and slid out of Tren. I allowed her to taste Daddy Dick. She wrapped both hands around Daddy Dick and she loved it. She gargled my shit and made my moans go inside Brittany as I was still feasting.

Brittany screams, "I wanna taste that Daddy Dick too!"

She climbed her way down and both girls got a taste of Daddy Dick. I had a view of two women fighting and wrestling over my dick like two pit bulls fighting over a steak.

Not really giving a damn right now because both were spinning their tongue around on my shit and it felt so damn good. Just like that, I pulled away from them both. They followed Daddy Dick like a newborn looking for their momma's nipple.

Two women pleasing me, too weird, I couldn't have two women pleasing me, shit not even one, I'm Dr. T, and I do the pleasing.

"Brittany?"

"Yes, Dr. T."

"Bend your fine ass over."

"Yes sir."

"What you want me to do Dr.T?" Tren asked.

"Come here and bend over." I gave that Asian ass a smack.

"Now go feed Brittany."

"Oh my God." Moaned Brittany, who couldn't reallu focus on Tren's pussy in her face right now because of Daddy Dick going in and out of her.

I took my hands and put a dip in Brittany's back and continued pushing Daddy Dick inside her.

"Dr. T, I love this Daddy Dick, keep giving me this Daddy Dick!"

"Ask and you shall receive. How does Daddy Dick feel?"

"He feels soooo dammmmmmnnn gooooood!"

"Ok, now shut up, babygirl trying to feed you."

"Yes sir."

"Can you taste babygirl?"

"Yes sir, she tastes good. Mmmmmm soooo gooood!"

Daddy Dick went deeper and deeper and both Brittany and Tren moaned out they were about to come. Faster and harder I went and finally, one hard thrust from Daddy Dick and we all came at the same time.

I start to put on my suit that Brittany ripped off of me and I saw two fine ass women I had right there with smiles on their faces. That's what it's all for, to see beautiful women, all women with smiles on their faces and with the '*I'm a queen bitch*' attitude.

Fully dressed and looking sharp once again I prepared to go home and meet up with Maria.

"Brittany, it was great seeing you again. And Tren it was my pleasure meeting you."

"The pleasure was all mine Dr. T," Tren said with a finger in her mouth and still looking at my crotch.

"Thanks for everything Dr. T, I really needed that."

"I know Brittany, and it's no problem at all. I'll see you later."

Simultaneously they say, "Bye Dr. T!"

"Tren, don't tell anybody about this."

"I won't, but Brittany I gotta ask you something. Uhhh........."

"Yes Tren, Daddy Dick was talking to you?"

Chapter 9

Stepping out of Shania's, all I could think about was, damn what a day and it's still not over with, I had to meet up with Maria in a lil' bit.

I couldn't help but wonder why JB thought I was always with Maria; she knew I didn't want her like that. Shit, but don't get me wrong, Maria is a beautiful woman, but she's not who I want to settle down with or have I ever thought of her like that. Instantly, Patrice popped into my mind. She's definitely an interesting lady and I have to see how that booty works.

I was laughing to myself, but seriously Patrice was definitely someone I wanted to get to know. I took out my phone and dialed Maria's number.

"Hello, this is Maria."

"Why you answer the phone like that when you know damn well it's me?"

"Hey Dr. T!" Just like that, Maria went from answering the phone all business like to talking all sexy and shit.

As bad as I wanted to make her laugh right now, I just couldn't. Maria was the type that I just had to keep it straight and to the point, but something was telling me she was in need of some laughs today.

"Now you trying to talk all sexy and shit, damn girl, got my dick hard already and you really ain't said too much of nothing."

"Dr. T you so crazy." Maria said laughing.

"Did you still want me to come over tonight?"

"Yea, I sense that you need to. Meet me at my house in about an hour." That gave me time to clean myself up before she got there.

Still, I couldn't help but to keep thinking about Patrice and how I'm going to tell her about this Dr. T shit. I'm sure she'll understand, yea right. Once again, I took out my phone, but this time I call up JB.

"What up Terry?"

"Nothing much JB, what you up to?"

"Shit, I just got through calling my wife and pulling some ol' Dr. T shit on her, and you were right. She told me to be ready for her when she gets home. Yea boy. How about you, how did that break room thing go?"

"Trust me, you don't wanna know."

"Damn, like that?"

"Yea man, and get this, while I'm doing Brittany's ass, an Asian chick walks her ass up in there and start stroking my back."

"Damn, I know Brittany selfish ass wasn't having that huh?"

"Not at first but she..."

"Nigga you had a threesome with them didn't you?"

I was no longer able to hold it in, but I didn't call JB to talk about Brittany and Tren, I needed some advice on how to tell Patrice about Dr. T. Staying quiet for a little while longer, then finally saying "Yea man, I did."

"Dr. Muthafuckin T, you my idol man. Teach me man, teach me!"

"JB you crazy, but listen, some other stuff happened at Shania's after you left and I need your advice on something."

Shocked and excited, JB blurted out, "What....Dr. T needs advice from lil ol' me?"

"Come on man, I'm serious."

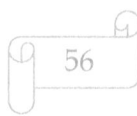

"Aight, what's up Terry," JB said quickly changing his tone.

"I met this woman at Shania's and we hit it off pretty good, I let her read some of my poems........"

"Aww shit, did Dr. T get her too." JB said, not knowing what I'm getting at.

"Naw man, that's the thing. I sat there and watched her for a while before I even approached her, and you know if Dr. T sees something in need of him, he acts on it ASAP. But I didn't think she was in need of me, I was in need of her."

"What you trying to say Terry." JB said with a confused tone in his voice.

"I'm saying that me, Terry, is digging this girl, it has nothing to do with Dr. T....kinda."

"Soooo....Terry, what's the problem?"

"Dr. T is the problem. This woman could possibly be someone I would want to date, but I need your advice on how I'll tell her about Dr. T because you know she ain't gon' be down with that."

"Terry, man listen, I'ma keep it real with you; you just met her, there's no need to start thinking about she's the one and all that shit man. Just let whatever happen, happen. I'm sure you will know when the perfect time to tell her, that's even if you will have to. Just enjoy talking to her on the phone and going on dates, then when you see things starting to get serious, you just gon' have to man up and tell her the truth."

JB joked around a lot, but he knew when I needed him to be serious. He knew I was probably looking way past this woman and just seeing a wife and kids. He's right though, I only had one conversation with Patrice.

"You're right JB. I'll just let whatever happens, happen."

"Good, ya'll going out tonight?"

"Naw man, Maria supposed to be coming over."

I just knew he was about to eat this up.

"Ohhhh right, Maria. That's who you gonna end up with. Not this Patrice lady."

"Whatever man, let me go wash myself up before she gets here."

"Aight man, I'll let you slide this time, but seriously, remember what I said about your Dr. T situation."

"Right on, I appreciate it man, now go enjoy a night with wifey."

"Yeeeaaaaa buddy!"

I rushed up inside my house and toss my keys somewhere. Lit some candles, took out a bottle of wine and put on some music, all while undressing.

I walked around the house butt ass naked with my dick just hanging. I hopped in the shower and this time, I thought about something Natalie said while I was on the phone with Maria, "Does Dr. T know?"

That's something I'm going to have to explore tonight, but damn this shower feels good. Visions of me and Patrice in this shower begin to fill my head. I can see myself making love to her right now in this shower.

Shit, I need to get her off my mind. Her wet, long black hair that laid on her back and her smooth, slippery, caramel skin is all I could see right now, not to mention her pointy nipples that's begging me to suckle upon thee.

Damn, she making me get all Shakespearish now, shit. Ok, let me hurry up because Maria will be here soon. Finishing up my shower and drying off, I put on some of my Issie Miyake cologne and threw on some Joe boxers and a wife beater. This is chill mode for me, Maria wouldn't mind.

While I was waiting on Maria, one of my favorite songs came on and I got to singing Tyrese's,

Signs of Love Making.
"I'm a Capricorn, I came here to get manish, oooh I know it's good when you start speaking Spanish. Airy, sexually, you full of energy, after I'm done, you still telling me you want me. I met a Gemini, ooooh what a sex drive, she wanted it from the front, back, left and the right. Baby I will guarantee, to give you everything ya body is missing; these are the signs of love making."

Damn, that's my shit. I heard my door bell ring, so I strutted on over there and opened up.

Chapter 10

"Hey babygirl, come on in here."

"Hey Dr. T, you look mighty comfortable Papi."

She walked by and I was dazed by her scent, but of course I couldn't do that with Maria. I already know she wanted me for herself, even though she's married.

So I have to keep all the mushy shit to a minimum with her. We walked over to the den and I offered Maria a drink as she sat down.

"Yea, I'll take whatever you have. Dr. T, can I ask you something?"

"You ask me that every time you see me," that's what I wanted to say, but I'll play nice tonight.

"Yea, what is it gorgeous?" I walked back over to her with two glasses and a bottle of wine.

Maria had her head down as if she was in deep thought while Tony Toni Tone, *Lay Your Head on My Pillow*, played in the background.

"I just want to know how long do you plan on doing this Dr. T thing, I mean, you have to want somebody........?"

"Maria, what have I told you?"

"Yea, I know not to question things that can't be explained, but I'm not asking you to explain, I'm just asking to see what you want."

I was in shock because why would someone actually care about what I wanted. She did come here for me; I knew deep down this visit was about Maria.

She either have something deep to tell me or she's stalling, trying to brace herself for this Daddy Dick.

"Maria?"

"Yes, Dr. T?"

"How was your day?" I had to always control things with Maria because she controled every other aspect of her life.

"Dr. T I just wanted to......" "Maria!" I screamed again.

"We are not going to play this game again. We can sit here and talk politics, sports, world hunger, and business, all that, it doesn't really matter to me, but this is not the time to try and get into my head. You seem to have a lot of tension Maria, what's wrong?"

Every meeting with Maria was not about Daddy Dick, sometimes she just had some things on her mind and she somehow considered me a therapist and told me her problems and hoped I have a solution for them.

"Well Dr. T, you know I often look at my life and try to get some kind of direction with everything. I'm just not happy right now. The man I'm in love with doesn't love me back and I don't know why. I have all the money in the world, and I'm still not happy."

I took my fingertips and slowly massaged Maria's scalp, trying my best to get her to relax. I wanted to just blurt out and ask her, why she thought her husband no longer loved her, but I decided against it

"Keep going baby love, Dr. T is here to listen to you."

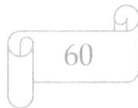

"Dr. T, I just don't get it, I think I'm a very attractive woman, I don't have any kids, I got money. Why is love staying away from me, can you answer that for me? I give my all to this man and he constantly makes me regret it!"

"Maria, baby?"

"Yes?"

"I'm going to tell you something Marvin Gaye said ok?"

"Ok Dr. T, what did he say?"

"He said, *'giving yourself to me, can never be wrong, if the love is true'* so giving yourself, all of yourself to your husband, is something you shouldn't regret, not if you truly feel your love for him is true. Just change the way you look at things and things will change."

"What do you mean by that Dr. T?"

"I mean, instead of thinking everything is bad right now, just think of this as the journey you have to go through to get where you want to be. If you don't enjoy the journey, you won't appreciate your destination. But love, you have to be true to yourself and be true in what you want and things will work out for the best."

I poured the both of us another glass of wine and wiped the tears from Maria's eyes. That had to be a no-no. Dr. T's weakness was tears. That's one thing that made Dr. T normal; it will make Terry come out and start going into my shit, and that's a no-no, a hell no.

"Come on babe, stop that crying. Like I said, you just have to be true to yourself. We all have needs and wants, but sometimes our needs and wants are the same thing and sometimes it's something you don't really need. Just always be true, and you won't ever get caught up in that situation."

"Dr. T, I have to tell you something, and it's kinda important Papi." Shit, I loved when she called me Papi.

"Does this have anything to do with what you and Natalie were talking about?"

"You heard us?"

"All I heard was Natalie asking you if I knew."

"Well, I don't really know how to tell you. You have to understand my intentions are not to hurt you or anything like that."

Ok. This is not good. A million things entered my mind and they were all unfinished thoughts. I tried desperately to figure it out before she told me, just so it wouldn't hurt as bad, if it hurt at all.

"Babygirl, just tell me. That's the best way to do it. Just say it, I'm just Dr. T, I'm not the police or nothing like that."

"Well Dr. T, I haven't been true to myself and maybe what you said is right. Maybe until I be true to myself, things will always be wrong."

Maria sat up and looked me dead in my eyes and then dropped her head like a kid that knows they're in trouble.

"Baby just tell me."

"Dr. T.......I........I.....I......I'm no longer married. I haven't been married for a while now. I know I lied to you about being married, but I thought that would make it easier for me to keep myself from falling for you, but it didn't. I'm in love with you Dr. T and I have been for some time now."

I was ok, because I've been lied to many a time before, so that's no big deal. I didn't understand why that was so hard for Maria to tell me. I could see if we were actually dating, then yea, there would be a reason for me to be pissed. But I felt nothing.

Ok, I'm not being true to myself, I'm fucking pissed right now. All I wanted to say was get the fuck up out my house you lying muthafucka. But I held it down and calmed myself down by finishing off my glass of wine and went to get some a little stronger like some Brandy. I threw back a couple of shots of that and then went back to Maria.

"Uhhhhh, yeaaa, uummm. Shit girl. You lied to me huh? Why in the hell did you think you had to lie to me? You could've still been getting this Daddy Dick; you didn't have to lie, fuck. What did you think telling me the truth would do? Have me say, 'ok, I know you lied and all, but the truth is I love you too' fuck naw!"

"Dr. T calm down....."

"Fuck that, you can't tell me this shit and then tell me to calm down. Get the fuck up out my house Maria!"

"Dr. T, you asked me to be truthful and I had to tell you beca........."

"GET....THE....FUCK...OUT... OF MY...HOUSE....MARIA!"

"I'm sorry, I lied Dr. T, but like I said, I thought lying would keep me from this situation, me falling for you."

"Maria, can you please leave? I need you to leave right now. I can't talk about this right now, not now, please leave!"

"I'll leave if you tell me we can talk later."

I grabbed her things and walked and talked on my way to the door. One thing I couldn't tolerate was lying. I guess that's why I've been stressing over how I would tell Patrice about Dr. T. Lying was not an option.

"Maria, we'll talk about this later, bye."

I damn near booted her off my porch and went back and dealt with the truth Maria told me and drowned myself in the remains of my Brandy.

Chapter 11

I woke up alone again in my bed with an empty Brandy bottle lying next to me. I was confused over what I thought was a nightmare, but I knew it was all reality.

I knew I probably said some harsh things to Maria when she was just telling me the truth that was in her heart. I just couldn't accept the fact that I keep getting lied to. I'm Dr. T, I do everything to make this woman feel like a princess and she felt the need to lie to me.

Once again, I walked around my house butt ball naked like it was the normal thing to do and head toward the shower with my dick flopping from thigh to thigh.

I turned on the shower and made it burning hot and sat down in the tub to allow the hot water to sooth my brain. I was relaxed thought about last night again. I couldn't help but think that somehow this was my fault. If I was doing everything right, Maria wouldn't have felt that she needed to lie to me, but what more could I have done?

With all this that has happened; this hot ass water was making me slowly forget about it with every drop of water that touched my body. It sent me into total relaxation.

I tilted my head down so it could receive the bulk of the water and somehow massage all that shit out of my head. I continued to relax for about another hour, thoughtless.

Once out of the shower, I walked around naked allowing my cool air conditioned home to dry me off instead of the drying towels. I grabbed my phone off my leather loveseat that somehow was able to soak up all those tears that Maria shed.

On my phone, there were 10 missed calls, 7 new voicemails and 6 text messages, all from Maria. I cleared all that out without returning calls, listening to or reading messages.

I grabbed the piece of paper that Patrice wrote her phone number on and dialed the number. It just rung, so I hung up without leaving a voicemail. Just as I hung up, I saw her calling back.

"Hello?"

"Yes, did someone call Patrice?"

All cool and calm and shit, trying to hide my excitement for hearing her voice again, I say "Hey Patrice, this is Terry, we met at Shania's."

"Hey Terry, can I call you back in a minute?"

Well damn, was what I thought, if that's not a clear sign she wasn't interested, I don't know what was.

I was caught off guard by her response.

I lost all coolness and stuttered, "Uhh, ohhh, yeeaaaa, I'll talk to you later."

"Ok, bye Terry."

I heard a click sound before I even get a chance to say bye. I was left just staring at my phone butt as naked thinking what the hell just happened.

Sometimes you just get in the mode that you just need to talk to somebody. This situation right here was what made me envy JB so much. I couldn't see being in his situation and wanting to be away from my family like he does. Maybe I'm made to not wanting to be alone. I had this huge house and no one to share it with.

Just like that I started questioning myself, wondering if me and Maria could be together. Shaking my head, I walked to my room to throw on some shorts, not bothering to put on some boxers first. I decided to call up Maria and talk to her, really to apologize for how I acted; with the phone barely ringing once, Maria answered.

"Dr. T, is this you?"

"Hi Maria, I just want you to know that I thought about a lot since yesterday and I want to apologize to you."

"You...apologize....to me?" Maria asked as if an apology from me just doesn't exist in this world.

"Yes, Maria. I didn't handle my actions the best way. Don't get me wrong, I'm still mad and upset, but I still shouldn't have disrespected you the way that I did. I know you were basically doing what I was telling you to do, which is be true to yourself. Now I have to be true with you. Maria, I honestly don't believe you are in love with me. I don't see how you can possibly be in love with me. I mean, I don't do anything for you but fuck you. I think you are in love with Daddy Dick. I don't romance you, I don't surprise you, and I don't allow you to get inside my mind. So seriously, why do you think you are in love with me? Not to mention, if you are really in love with me, why have you referred so many ladies to me. Also, why did you feel you needed to lie to me about being married?"

I had a lot of questions for Maria, but these are things I really needed to know and maybe her answering these questions would make her feel better as well.

"Well Papi, I accept your apology. I know you were upset and I would have been too, but Papi I do know I love you. I referred all those women to you for the same reason I lied to you about being married. I thought it would keep me thinking of you as Dr. T, the man that made me feel happy about myself and hoped it continued having me think you were untouchable, but it didn't work. And yes, I am in love with Daddy Dick, shit I love me some Daddy Dick! Papi, you're right, you didn't do anything for me, you didn't romance me, surprise me, or any of that kind of stuff."

Still agitated because she still hasn't told me why she was in love with me. I took the phone away

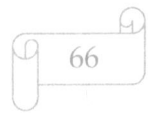

from my ear in frustration for a second then I
interrupted Maria.

"Maria! What did I do for you to fall in love
with me?"

"Papi, I fell in love you because of how Dr. T
cared so much. I love how he cares so much to put
women's needs to feel like a woman above his own
needs. That says so much of the kind of man you are."

I felt the need to burst her bubble by letting her
know that I was interested in someone else, but from
the way Patrice brushed me off the phone a few minutes
ago, I decided against it.

"Papi, that's why I fell in love, I tried many
times telling my heart not to fall for you, but for some
reason, my heart just doesn't do what I tell it to. My
mind and my heart are not in sync with each other."

"Maria, your mind can't tell your heart what to
do and you heart can't tell you mind what to think, but
sometimes you can let your mind not listen to your
heart and the other way around. I'm sure your mind was
telling you not to go there with me."

"Yea Papi, but my heart wanted you."

"Maria, you ignored your mind and forced your
heart to fall for me because it was something you
desperately wanted. Am I right? You desperately
wanted to love, and you desperately wanted to love me
because I was there."

Through all the sniffles and fallen tears, I could
tell something was really going on with Maria. Of all
people, I knew how it felt to want something so bad and
it just continued to run from you.

"Stop crying gorgeous."

"Papi, can I still see you when I need you?"

That wass the question I so badly wanted to
dodge.

"Maria, with you falling in love with me and
knowing that I don't feel the same about you, do you
really think that's a good idea for us to keep seeing each
other?"

I heard more cries from Maria and knew she
was taking it hard, but I had to be honest with her. As
much as she loves some Daddy Dick, it would just be

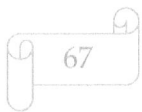

wrong for both of us to continue on with the arrangement.

I had to admit that I loved her shit too. Her pussy held onto Daddy Dick perfectly and it's juicy, just the way I like it.

I once had a nickname for her called Drip-Drip. But I had to put away those thoughts now, because continuing to sleep with Maria, knowing she's in love with me is doing no good for her, and that's what Dr. T is all about, doing the good for the queens.

"Ok Papi, I have to go, I'm sorry for everything, but I can't talk anymore....Bye."

"Maria......Maria......Hello, Maria?"

That's how it ended with Maria, but I knew that's not the last time I would hear from her. Maria had a lot of money and she's used to getting what she wants. So I know I will hear from again.

Chapter 12

"Hello?"

"Damn girl, it's about time, where the hell you been at. I been blowing up yo' phone and I know you been getting my messages?"

"Who is this?" Maria said, sounding like she'd been stuck in the bed the last couple of days.

"Girl, this is Nat. Maria, what's wrong with you? You been crying?"

"No, I'm sitting here with a big smile on my face. Do you want to know why?"

"Uumm, inquiring minds wanna know?"

"Well Nat, I have a huge smile on my face and I'm the happiest woman in the world because a friend of mine fronted me out about being in love with some nigga named Dr. T, and not only did she front me out, she convinced me to tell him that I'm in love with him."

With proud excitement in her voice Natalie screamed.

"Girl, that's good, I told you that!" Maria interrupted.

"Wait Nat, let me finish. This friend of mine convinced me to tell him I'm in love with him and I actually did it and guess what?"

"What girl?" Nat screamed, oblivious to the fact that Maria is about to go off on her.

"He cursed me the fuck out and....and....and kicked me out his house. Oh yea, he has no plans of seeing me again. So thank you for that Nat, because I was really getting tired of Dr. T." Maria said sarcastically.

"Maria, I'm sorry."

"Sorry, you're sorry. That's all you have to say, you're sorry. It's my fault for ever listening to you in the first place. I would probably have that Daddy Dick inside me right now if it wasn't for you!"

"Be careful girl. I know you're hurting and all that, but if you keep talking to me like that then we definitely gon' have a problem. Plus you mad at the wrong person. You are the one that lied to Dr. T about still being married. Shit you even lied to me about it. You can blame me all you want but he was going to figure it out one way or another. The question is what you gonna do about it because I know you not just gonna give up like that?"

Still lying in the bed in her night gown refusing to get up, Maria sniffed and started back crying realizing she has no plan in order to get Dr. T back or let alone....Daddy Dick.

"Nat, I don't know what I'm going to do. He don't want to see me anymore." A number buzzed in on Natalie's phone, but she ignored it and continued listening to Maria.

"It's all my fault, I should have just told him truth and maybe things would be different."

"Maria, what did he have to say?"

"He didn't have nothing to say, he just kicked me out his house once I told him I was no longer married and I had fallen in love with him. He did call me this morning though apologizing for the way he acted last night. And girl, that's the very reason I fell in love with him, because of his heart. He didn't have to call me and apologize for that. How many men out here will actually apologize for something like that?" Maria said as she wiped her tears away.

Natalie's phone buzzed again and she saw Dr. T's number come up on the caller ID, she had to interrupt Maria and let her know.

"Wait, Maria.....This is Dr. T buzzing in on the other line. Do you want me to answer it?"

"What, I wonder why he's calling you?"

"I don't know."

"Yes, go ahead and answer and call me right back to tell me what he wanted."

"Ok."

"This is Natalie."

"Hey Natalie, this is Dr. T. How are you doing beautiful?"

"I'm doing good Dr. T, how are you?" Natalie said, trying her best to play it cool, but she forgot who she was talking to....Dr. T.

"Could be better. Listen Natalie, I know you were probably on the other line with Maria, so I'll make this quick. Some things happened with me and Maria and I don't think that I'll be seeing her anymore, but now knowing how she feels about me, I don't think it's best for you and I to continue sleeping together. You may agree with me since that is your friend, but I just won't feel right sleeping with you knowing that Maria, your friend, is in love with me. Maria is a special woman and I hate all of this had to happen and I wish her all the best, but I just felt I needed to call you and tell you myself."

"That's fine Dr. T. Trust me, I completely understand. Just know that the one session we did have has changed my life, I have so much confidence in myself and I have you to thank for that."

"Thanks for understanding gorgeous. Tell Maria I apologize for disrespecting her. Even though she lied to me, my intention was not to hurt her back."

"She knows that Dr. T. Thank you for calling me and I will tell her anyway."

"Thanks. Ok. Bye suga."

"Bye Dr. T."

Natalie, thought to herself, how the hell she got caught in the middle of all this while she calld Maria back.

"Hello?"

"Hey girl, it's me."

"What did Dr. T have to say?" Maria asked, sounding like a kid back in elementary school having Natalie be the messenger girl.

"He just wanted to tell me that since you're in love with him, he won't feel right giving me that good Daddy Dick anymore. He also wanted me to tell you he apologizes for disrespecting you, his intentions were not to hurt you."

Left quiet on the phone, Maria again realizes this is the reason why she's in love with Dr. T. She lays in her bed, half listening to Natalie talk and half staring out into space.

"Hello......Maria......Hello...?"

"Yes, I'm here. I'm just thinking, trying to figure out what I'm going to do because, I am not letting this man out of my life. I love him Nat."

"Ok, good, do you need my help with anything?"

"No mami, I have to do this myself, but I will keep you updated on my progress."

"Just be careful and make sure that there's not another woman in the picture, I'll talk to you later." Not having thought about that. Maria had another reason to think of why Dr. T didn't want to be with her.

"I will girl, but I definitely don't care about another woman. I'll keep in touch with you. Bye Nat."

Chapter 13

I woke up in the middle of the night and found myself just laying in my huge California king size bed all alone with nothing on but some basketball shorts. I felt an emptiness that was horribly massaging my body.

I still couldn't help but to think about Maria and anticipate what our next encounter would be like. I knew she wasn't giving up on what she wanted. Who knows what could have happen between me and Maria in a different situation.

She was gorgeous, inside and out and not to mention she had a good thing in between her legs. Clearly, I was still buzzed from the couple of glasses of Alize that I drank before I went to bed. In the middle of my thoughts of Maria, I'm snapped out of it by the phone ringing; all I could think was Maria must be thinking of me also. It had to be her calling. I rolled over to see what time it was and my clock read 4:22 am. These are booty call hours; everybody knows that, so of course I will answered the phone.

"Hello?"

"Are you sleep?" a voice said, me not really recognizing it.

"Naw, I'm just sitting here thinking."

"Terry, do you even know who you're talking to?" I wanted to say, *hell naw, its 4:30 in the morning,* but I just took a wild guess.

"Is this Patrice?" I said, wishing it was.

"Yes Terry, this is Patrice. Look, I don't know why I'm calling, but I just felt I needed to call somebody and you came to mind."

Quickly, my emotions went from feeling like a little boy every time his first crush came around him to

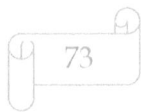

feeling something was wrong with someone that I may already have strong feelings for.

"Patrice, I'm glad I came to mind, but is everything ok?"

"Yea, it is, I just wanted to apologize for how I rushed you off the phone earlier, and I can imagine what you were thinking."

"That's ok beautiful, but are you sure everything is ok?"

"Not really Terry, I rushed you off the phone earlier because I had a lot going on. I'm at the hospital with my mom and she's not doing too good."

I listened to Patrice and I could tell she had been crying and all I wanted to do is be next to Patrice, hold her, comfort her and support her.

"Patrice, there's no need for you to apologize. I understand now you were not in a position to talk and I'm sorry to hear about your mom. Is there anything I can do?" I ask that question, but I knew that every time you ask somebody that question, the response is always nothing.

"Thanks for understanding Terry, but there's nothing you can do right now. Terry, I have to go, I just wanted to call you so you didn't think I was intentionally trying to be rude and plus I wanted to talk to you."

"No problem Babygirl. Patrice what hospital are you at?" Hearing tears flood over the phone. Patrice says, "I'm sorry Terry, I have to go" and she hung up.

I desperately needed to find out which hospital Patrice was at. I called the number back that she called from and luckily it was the hospital's number and the operator's voice says, "Henderson's Methodist Hospital."

I threw on some sweat pants and a sweat shirt; flipped on my Jordan cap, brushed my teeth and dabbed on some cologne. I grabbed my keys off the counter and rush to my BMW, set the navigation system to Henderson's Methodist Hospital. I just hope nothing has gone wrong with Patrice's mom.

I lost my parents in a car accident when I was three years old and not a day goes by I don't think about them or want to talk to them. So I could imagine how hurt Patrice would be. Quickly, I cleared my mind of anything negative.

I sped through yellow lights and ran stop signs. I was shocked there wasn't a cop around, but I probably would have kept driving and explained why when I got to the hospital. As soon as I pulled into the parking lot, my phone started ringing. I was too discombobulated, I fumbled around with it until I finally answered.

"Hello, Hello, Patrice? Patrice is everything ok?"

"Dr. T?"

Knowing Patrice had no idea who Dr. T was, I just thought to myself awwww shit.

"Maria, is this you?"

"Yes Papi, I couldn't sleep and I wanted to hear your voice, who is Patrice?"

"Maria is everything ok?" I asked before I get off the phone with her.

"Yes, I just need to hear your voice, Dr. T who is Patrice?"

"Ok Maria, I'm gonna have to call you back, I'm in the middle of something very important."

"Uh........ummmm....ok Papi, goodnight."

I hung up and rushed into the hospital. I ran around desperately trying to find Patrice. Stopping and looking around, I turned my head and there sat Patrice all alone with her hands on her head. Slowly I approach her as if I knew something bad has already happened. I take my hand and rub her back and softly whisper.... "Patrice.......Patrice........?." I continued to call her name and she was in a world of her own which was understandable. Finally, she moaned words I couldn't understand.

"Patrice, did you say something?" She raised her head up and I saw a pair of beautiful eyes that were all cried out and. She leaned her head on my shoulder covering her face. I couldn't do nothing but hold her and comfort her.

"Why is all this happening," Patrice asked softly. I remembered the phrase I use for Maria.

"I've learned never to question things that can't be explained. Just put it in God's hands and whatever decision he makes will always be the right one."

"Terry, I just can't live without my mom, I just can't do it." Patrice said, still crying with her head buried in my chest.

"How is she doing?"

"The doctors are in with her now and they tell me it's not looking too good."

"Do you mind me asking what's wrong?"

"Still crying, Patrice pauseed and said, "My mom has lung cancer, she's lost a lot of weight and she barely recognizes me. They had to take her off the breathing machine earlier and now it's just a matter of time."

"Terry, I just don't understand why this is happening to me, I do things the right way, I go to church, I do community charity work, I give back, I'm saving myself til' marriage and nothing good happens to me, now my mother will be taken away from me."

I missed everything she said after 'saving myself til marriage.' After thinking about her being a virgin, the doctor came and interrupted my thoughts.

"Excuse me, Mr. ?"

"Davis, I'm Mr. Davis and she's Ms. Williams. Doctor, please tell me you have some good news?"

"I'm afraid not Mr. Davis. I don't think Ms. Williams has too much longer and I think you guys should call your family to say your goodbyes; again, I'm very sorry. Her eyes are still open and she may still be able to speak."

"I'm the only family she has." Patrice interrupted

"Patrice are you sure, there's no one else you need to call?"

"I said I'm the only family she has!" Being yelled at by Patrice definitely caught me off guard but I understood what she was feeling.

"Well Ms. Williams feel free to go ahead and say your goodbyes, if you need anything let me know and again I'm sorry." Dr. Mitchell walked away, Patrice started crying and I felt so helpless. She stood and stared at the door.

"Terry, I don't think I can do this." She cried.

"Babygirl, I know it's hard but you have to do this, you have to go see your mom."

"Terry." Patrice held her hand out.

"Yes Patrice?"

"Can you come with me?"

I was just as scared and nervous as Patrice was.

This will be the memory of the first time I meet her mom. I was hoping more for a meeting over dinner and a night full of laughs, but those types of things is what people take for granted, the meeting of people, they are so precious and most of the time we don't even realize it.

"Yes Patrice, I'll come with you."

I took her hand and slowly opened the door for Patrice to walk through. I watched the moment Patrice and her mom had together and it brought tears to my eyes.

"Ohhhhhh baby, wash them tears away from your eyes." her mom said with a slow struggled voice.

"Baby, God jus' says that it's my time."

"Mom, what am I supposed to do without you?

I've been with you every single day of my life and I can't go on without you, I just can't. Who's gonna crack jokes about the way I dance? Who's gonna help me prepare dinner like we always do together? Who will tell me how bad I was as a little girl?"

"Stop that baby; I will always be here with you. You will have the memory of me."

"Mom I don't want memories if you're no longer here to make more of them, I want you here to make more memories with me!"

"I won't argue with God's decision baby."

"Then I'll do it, I'll argue with Him. How could He take you away from me right now, it's not fair!"

I walked over to Patrice and her mom and saw a beautiful lady. She had veins filled with pain and loss of her hair to go along with the slenderness of her body and yet she still praised God and still possesses a beautiful smile.

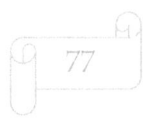

Patrice held her mom's hand, kissed and placed it to her heart.

"Patrice, your mom will always be in your heart and God understands your anger and you know He won't put you through anything you can't handle. This is a time to say goodbye, not fill your heart with hate toward a Man your mom will be spending all of eternity with, God."

"I love you mom, and I will miss you."

Her mom gasped for air and struggled to speak.

"I love you too baby, always."

She saw me and amazingly she managed to smile at me and say, "Take good care of my baby."

Slowly her eyes began to close and her smile was just a little less now. Those six words were the last words Patrice's mom would speak.

Patrice kissed her mom on her cheek and once more on her hand. The doctors walked in as we walked out and Patrice grabbed hold of my hand and we both cried as we left Henderson's Methodist Hospital.

Chapter 14

As Patrice and I left the hospital, I wondered what was going through her head. Was it making the necessary funeral arrangements? Or was it pain and shock? Maybe she was thinking why in the hell I came here.

She clinched my hand and held it tighter and tighter showing power in such a soft touch. Patrice's hair was blowing as she snuggled up against me to stay warm as if the sweat pants and sweatshirt wasn't enough to do the job. I looked at Patrice and she looked back, allowing me to wipe away her tears.

"Patrice, where did you park?"

Wiping her eyes and sniffing she said, "I took a cab here. My car is in the shop with engine problems or something like that."

"Well it's almost 8:00, do you want to go eat breakfast with me, if not, I can definitely understand."

"That'll be fine Terry."

When we got to my car, I opened the door for her and she gave me a weird piercing look. She gave me the same look when put her seat belt on for her.

We had a quiet drive over to Mother's Breakfast Place. No words really had to be said because I

understood her not wanting to talk and she understood me not knowing what to say.

Finally we arrived and was seated.

"Hello, welcome to Mother's Breakfast, my name is Jon and I'll be your waiter. Can I start you guys off with something to drink?"

"Patrice, do you know what you want to drink?" Silence…

Not wanting to just sit there with a blank look on my face, I try to remain cool as always, so I've been told.

"Jon, can you just bring me raspberry lemonade and a pitcher of orange juice?"

"Got it, I'll be right back with your drinks."

"Thanks."

I was looking over the menu, but I already knew what I wanted. I glanced at Patrice every couple of seconds and finally ask her, "Do you want to leave, we don't have to stay?"

"I'm sorry Terry, we can stay, I'm just thinking about a lot right now."

"I know babygirl, do you wanna talk about it?"

Trying hard to avoid it, Patrice smiled.

"I like it when you call me Babygirl. Will you believe it if I told you no one has ever given me a nick name?"

"Naw, I can't believe that. Well there's a first for everything right?"

"Yes, I have a lot of first that's waiting on me."

"Oh yea, you feel like sharing them with me?"

She blushed so hard that her caramel cheeks turned red.

"You're really gonna make me do this aren't you Terry?"

"Yes Maam!"

"Ok, some of my first awaiting is, to get married, have kids, and visit another country."

"So, you gonna keep all the juicy stuff to yourself huh?" We both laughed hard at my attempts to dig deep for some good stuff. Jon finally arrived with our drinks.

"Here you guys go, your raspberry lemonade and pitcher of orange juice. Are you ready to order?"

"Babygirl you ready to order?"

"Yea, I'll take the two pancake meal with my eggs scrambled, thanks."

"Jon, I'll have the usual."

"Anything else?"

"Nope, that will be it."

"Ok, I'll be back shortly with your order."

"Sooo, Terry you come here often huh?"

"Yea, I do. Can I ask you a question Patrice?"

"Yes, sure."

"When we were walking to my car and I opened your door for you, you gave me a look. What was that look for?"

"Well Terry, you have to understand something. I've had relationships but I haven't had relationships, I know that sounds confusing. What I mean is, I only read about people like you."

"Care to explain?"

"Well for one, you not only came to see me here in the hospital, but you found out which hospital I was at, you opened my car door. Shit, you even put my seat belt on for me. In my world, men like you don't exist. I have to read about you or see it on TV. Now, honestly I do know men like you exist, but never thought one would be in my presence. You open up doors for me. I've only seen my Dad treat my mom that way."

"Is your Dad still here?"

I knew the answer to that since her dad wasn't with her at the hospital, but I could be wrong, maybe he was still here just not a part of their lives.

"No he died when I was 11 years old and I had my mom to help me get through it, but who will help me get through this one?"

"You know I'm here."

"Yea, I know it now. Are your parents still here?"

"Naw my parents died when I was three years old and my grandma raised me until she died when I was 18 and I've been on my own ever since then. In some ways I'm like you, I'm the only child, didn't have

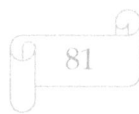

a big family so there wasn't anyone to get me through it. Maybe we can start to be there for each other."

"I would like that! I will tell you that I'm not an only child, but that's a long conversation for another day."

"Good, so would I. Well babygirl, we can talk about that anytime you want. Do you mind if I ask you some more questions?"

"No, go right ahead and make sure you get them all out because I have some for you too." She said smiling.

"Well, not really questions, but I just want to get to know you."

"Are you shy Mr. Davis?" Patrice asked with a sarcastic look on her beautiful face.

"No, that's what's so funny. Excuse me if I'm too forward or out of line when I say this, but I just love to look at you. You have the most beautiful eyes I have ever seen and your smile just makes everything around me go numb."

"Terry, if your Dad wasn't around, who taught you to be such a smooth talker? My mom warned me about slick talking guys like you?" Little does Patrice know, I'm like no other guy she could make up herself.

"What are guys like me, if you don't mind me asking?"

"Well, you seem to be telling me all the right things and doing all the right things. What do you want from me?" I wanted so bad to say I'm Dr. T and I know exactly what to do and to say to make a woman feel like she's the queen of the world, but this was different.

I like this girl and even though Dr. T's feelings come natural to my clients, it's also natural to Patrice.

The truth of it all is that I do those things, the opening of doors, the compliments to her without knowing what I'm doing or that I'm doing it.

"I guess I've seen so many women end up with bad guys. I've seen how bad these guys treated them that I learned very young to always make a lady feel good and make my feelings come natural and real, nothing fake. I like to know that you are smiling and you feel good about yourself. You asked what I want from you; all I want is for you to be happy. Period."

"Ok Mr. Serious I just wanted to know. After my dad died, my mom ended up with some bad guys and I always told myself I won't end up with guys like that, that only wanted one thing from me, so I made the decision not to have sex until I was married or until I know I have found the right guy."

"I think I'm the right guy."

"Of course you do Mr. Davis."

Patrice and I sat and talked for about another two hours and still continued to talk as I drove her home just enjoying the company of each other. I tried so hard to make Patrice's day as normal as possible with everything that had happened earlier. She's very interesting and I found myself falling, falling in very strong like for Patrice.

I like everything about her that I know of. I just love her long silky hair and the deepest brown eyes that I could just drown in. Patrice also has the softest skin that's softer than air and could melt away all the tension in my body just by a simple touch of her.

I couldn't help but to think that capturing the love of this woman was impossible because the need and the 'have to' to tell Patrice about Dr. T. I will tell her soon rather than later just so I won't waste our time.

Then there's the issue of Maria and knowing that will be a hard chapter to close because I know I have not heard the last of her.

Finally, we made it to Patrice's home, I felt bad that she now has to go to the home where her and her mom stayed together and pack up her mother's things.

"Well babygirl, I had fun with you today and I'm sorry about your loss."

"Thanks Terry for taking my mind away from it all, I needed it. I really enjoyed talking to you and in a way you have helped me."

"How is that?"

"I don't know how to explain it. It's like you knew when to talk about my mom and you knew when to make me laugh and cry. You just knew what to say and when to say it."

"Well babygirl, I'm a true believer in how and when you say something is just as important as what you say. Just know that it's ok to cry and I'm here for you anytime you need me. Just call on Terrrrrrry." I sung using Eryka Badu's melody to "Just call Tyrone."

Patrice couldn't help but laugh.

"See that's exactly what I'm talking about Terry, you make me laugh!"

"What, you didn't like my singing?"

"Loved it, well I'm gonna go up here and pack up my mom's things and get started on planning everything."

"Ok babygirl, do you need any help?"

"Of course, but I think I need to do this alone."

"So will I talk to you later?"

"I hope so." Patrice said as she kissed me on the cheek and walked away. I drove away like a teenager that couldn't wait to tell his best friend about his date. I'll call JB when I make it home, but I still owed Maria a phone call.

Chapter 15

I finally woke up from a long nap, which I was about due for since I had an up and down morning. I witnessed Patrice lose her mother, watched her break down and after all that, we spent some quality time together. I can already see that Patrice meant a lot to me.

I want to be everything she wants me to be for her. I've thought about making love to Patrice numerous of times. I've thought about feasting upon the sweet juices of Patrice and feeling myself inside her, but I also want to make love to her soul, her spirit.

I want what no other man has ever gotten from her, the chance for her to make love to me. I can't wait for Patrice to have Daddy Dick, her Daddy Dick, or whatever she wanted to call it. It's her's.

I wondered what Patrice was doing right now, I didn't want to call because I don't want to seem too pushy and I knew she was probably still packing. I pray she is doing ok, losing your parents is a hard thing to deal with and I definitely know the feeling.

I was only three when my parents died, but Granny always showed me some home videos of them so I will always know and remember what they look liked.

My mom was short and she was the most beautiful woman I had ever seen. Momma always had a

smile on her face and she just loved to laugh. Her voice was the sweetest thing ever to my ears and she always sung to me.

Tears started to fall from my eyes as I remembered my momma. Momma also had the most beautiful eyes that God has created. For some reason, I remember Momma always wore flower dresses and she loved to play with me all of the time.

Daddy was the complete opposite. He was a little taller than Momma, but he was the very serious type. I remember his strong hands and Granny caught him on tape being very soft and gentle while talking to me when I was sleep, he had no idea Granny was recording him and I'm glad she did.

"Wow, son you are getting big. Dad can't take his eyes off of you and I know you're sleep, but I wanted to come in and talk to you. You never know how many chances you will get in life to just look and talk to your loved ones. Son, never take life for granted and always, always treat women with respect. I love your momma so much, she's my queen. Even the times they are acting a little unlike themselves, still treat them like the 10s that God created them to be. You are my lil' man and I love you son, Goodnight."

Granny said that Daddy did that a lot. I miss them all like crazy, Momma, Daddy, and Granny. Daddy must of talked to me a lot about how to treat a woman. I wonder what he'd think about this Dr. T shit if he was still here.

Sometimes I also wonder what my mother would think. What about my life would be the same and what would be different? Would I be married with kids now? Like I've told Maria, don't question what can't be explained or changed.

I remember my dad saying something to me on tape, he said, "Son, everything in your life has already been planned out for you. You have a birth date and a death date, and you can't change any of that. Everything that will ever happen to you is supposed to happen, it's part of His plan and He never needs a Plan B. So don't worry about what's happened or what will happen, only thing you can control is how you come out of it. The way you handle certain situations shows your character."

While I was daydreaming about my lost loved ones, I felt my phone vibrate and hoped and prayed that it wasn't Maria because I really didn't have the energy to deal with her right now.

I saw JB's name appear on the caller ID and instantly I was like a teenage boy that couldn't wait to tell his best friend about his first date.

"Hello?"

"Come on man! It's just me. You don't have to put on the sexy Dr. T voice," JB said jokingly.

"What's up JB, how did the night go with wifey?"

"It went pretty damn good; I won't be surprised if she tells me she's pregnant in a couple of weeks, but anyway, on to the good stuff. What happened with Patrice? Did you tell her about Dr. T?" JB kept going on and on, question after question before I could even answer the first one.

"JB, a lot has happened in the last couple of days that I need to tell you about. Some good and some is just horrible."

Just like that, the tone in JB's voice changed. I didn't know what he was expecting to hear from me, but he was definitely concerned.

"Terry, is everything ok man? I mean seriously, nothing bad happened did it? Give me the bad first."

"I'm ok, but I guess I should start off by telling you that you was kind of right about Maria. She came over the other night when I left Shania's and man she told me some things that she just should have kept to herself."

"Ok Terry, so how did you react when she told you she loved you and wanted you?" I was caught off wondering how JB knew this without me telling him.

"JB, how did you know what was going on?" I asked while I got out of the chair to make me a Rum and Coke. JB joked around a lot, but when he does get serious, he's pretty cool to talk to.

"Terry, I tried to warn you about Maria. Anybody could see she was starting to get too attached to you, I could tell just by the stories you would tell me about her. And from what you told me about her, she seems that she is accustomed to getting what she wants, so the question or questions are, how did you handle it and what are you going to do about it?"

"Well man, the fact that Maria told me that she was in love with me is not all of it. She also lied about being married to her husband. I don't get why she felt she had to lie about it. I told her that she still could have been getting Daddy Dick. JB, I don't think I handled it too well, but I did call and apologize."

"Shit Terry, what did you do?"

"I just got pretty mad and raised my voice at her. Oh yea, and I kicked her out of my house. I have no idea what I'm going to do about this situation. I told Maria I think its best that we no longer continue to mess around with each other."

I lay back in my recliner knowing I still had to tell him about what I went through with Patrice, and instantly I started daydreaming about her not paying attention to what JB was saying. Instead I thought about the beautiful Patrice, how long her hair was, how soft her touch was, and how good her lips tasted.

Ok, all she did was kiss me on my cheek, but that is just how powerful it was. I find myself already missing her breathtaking smile, and falling in her deep caramel eyes.

"Hello, earth to Terry," JB screamed.

"My bad man, what did you say?"

"Terry what are you going to do about this, because from what you told me about Maria, I just can't see her going away quietly. I'll tell you one thing; you better figure it out before you and Patrice get any closer. Nigga, do I have to make you watch '*A Thin Line Between Love and Hate*', because as Martin Lawrence said in the movie, '*you will be caught up in a real life fatal attraction*!'

"JB, I don't know what I'm going to do, but I supposed to talk to Maria later on today, but that is not a conversation I'm looking forward to having. Ok, now I have to tell you about what happened with Patrice last night or early this morning."

"Shit nigga, don't tell me you already slept with Patrice, smooth ass Dr. T!"

I always thought JB loved my situation, because his eyes always lit up when I told him about a new girl. This was fine because I only wished I had his situation just as much as he wished he had mine.

"Naw man, it's not even about that yet with her. Anyway, I called her yesterday and she kind of rushed me off the phone. Then she called me back in the middle of the night to apologize. She said she had a lot of stuff going on and she was at the hospital with her mom, then she rushed off the phone again before I knew which hospital she was at. So to make a long story short, I found out which hospital she was at and drove there. I ended up being the last person her mom spoke to before she died."

"Damn Terry, that's sad man, what did her mom tell you?"

"She just told me to make sure I take good care of her baby and I plan to do just that. After we watched her mom take her last breath, I offered to take her to breakfast, just so she can clear her head a little bit and we just talked and really got to know each other."

"Terry, I know you don't want to hear this man, but it seems you are really falling for this girl and you have two things on you that can come bite you in the ass and mess everything up with you and Patrice. You have the Maria situation and this Dr. T shit that you need to tell Patrice about, my advice would be to shy away from Patrice a little bit until you figure out what you are going to do about it." JB had a good point, but I'll take care of this my way. I will talk to Maria later on and just tell her to leave me alone and hope she understands.

"Ok JB, I'll think about what you said, but for now I'm going to go prepare myself for this talk I have to have with Maria."

"Aight man, call me if you need me."

"Will do, talk to you later."

Chapter 16

After I got off the phone with JB, I sat back and tried to figure this out. With only some basketball shorts on, I walked over and made me a Rum and Coke hoping the answers to all my problems would be at the bottom of this liquor bottle, and I threw on some music just to have a moment to myself.

Just as I sat back down, my phone vibrated again and even though I was a little reluctant to answer it, I knew it was Maria wanting to have our talk. I knew it had to be on her time, why couldn't she have waited until I called her, but anyway I have me a nice little buzz right now so I figured I'll go ahead and get this talk out the way.

"Hello?" I said with a '*damn here we go tone*'.

I guess my buzz was a little better than I thought.

"Terry?" A beautiful voice said.

"Hello, Terry are you there?"

"Patrice is that you?"

"Yes Terry, it's me. What are you doing?"

"Nothing babygirl, I'm just listening to some music and having me a drink."

I tried my best to play my buzz off, but it wasn't working since I was caught off guard by Patrice's phone call.

"Are you having fun without me Mr. Davis?" Patrice asked jokingly.

"Not really, but I have been thinking about you."

"Oh really?"

"How could I not, you are a very interesting young lady Ms. Williams."

"Whatever drunky!"

"Ok Ms. Williams watch how you talk to drunk people, our feelings get hurt easily, then you will have to come over and make me feel all better, now you wouldn't want that would you?"

"Of course not." Patrice said with a sarcastic tone.

"Good."

"Well Terry, I called you because I wanted to say thanks again for last night and this morning. I just can't stop thinking about you."

"Well babygirl, I can't stop thinking about you either."

"What do you think about Terry?" Patrice asked, leaving me thinking about which direction I should take this.

"Babygirl, it's a lot of different things that I'm thinking. I've been wondering if you're doing fine over there. I've been thinking about your mom and I've been thinking about you."

"What about me Mr. Davis?" For some reason I just loved how Patrice called me Mr. Davis.

"Well Babygirl, I've been thinking about your lips. I was thinking out loud earlier and I thought I missed the way your lips taste and all you did was kiss me on my cheek."

"I guess I should say thank you, I never been complimented on my kisses."
"That's because you haven't been kissing the right person Babygirl."

"Is that what you think Terry?"

"Yes I do!"

"Ok Terry, what would be so different from kissing you compared to anyone else?"

Normally my response would be, I'm Dr. T, I know just where you want to be kissed and how you want to be kissed, but that's not what happened. This is weird because me, Terry, is shy and don't always know the right thing to say at the right time because I get nervous, but now was not the time to be nervous.

"Well babygirl, I could show you better than I can tell you, and I can't compare my kisses to anyone else's. Different people like different things, but you should know that kissing me will be an experience in itself because many men kiss to begin a sexual act. I kiss you to take your breath away, I kiss you to make all your worries and thoughts go away. I kiss you to make your body weak and I kiss you the way I will make love to you, my kisses will be making love Ms. Williams and seeing how you never made love before, I think we both can agree that my kisses don't compare to what you had before."

"You are such a smooth talker Terry, but in a good way. I have to tell you that you have my lips over here begging for a kiss now. How did you do that?"

"Do what Babygirl?"

"Well it actually felt like I was kissing you and just your words alone was better than any kiss I've had."

"Thank you Babygirl, but if you wasn't the woman you are, I wouldn't have been able to think of kissing you the way that I described."

"Terry?"

"Yes Babygirl?"

"When can I see you again?"

"How about tonight, your place?"

"Tonight is fine Terry, but can it be at your place, I really want to get out of this house?"

I could understand Patrice wanting to get out of her house, I'm sure she's been packing all day and steady thinking about her mom and making herself go crazy, but I can't help but imagine what a messed up night it would be if Maria decided she wanted to just pop up. That will be a risk I will be willing to take because I am in need of seeing Patrice.

"That's fine Babygirl, you can come around 8 o'clock."

"Ok Terry, can I ask a favor?"

"Yea?"

"Can you please tell me a poem?"

I laugh to myself because that's so out the blue and plus I was still a little tipsy. I wonder if she expects me to make one up.

"Sure babygirl, but would you like me to make one up or one that I already wrote?"

"I prefer you to make one up; I mean only if you can." Patrice said sarcastically, but she is about to see just how good I can be when I'm put on the spot, not to mention with some liquor still in my system.

"Ok, is there a special topic you wish to hear about Ms. Williams?"

"You can talk about anything you want to talk about Mr. Davis."

"Ok, I'll name this one *Rhythmic Senses of Love.*"

"I like the title Mr. Davis."

Rhythmic Sense of Love
We have a Rhythmic sense of Love
Only which you and I know of
The sweet touch of our bodies and sight of our silhouette
To your taste of my nectar and my feel of you wet
I make love to you emotionally and you make love to me
I speak to your heart and you seduce my mind sensually
You listen to the vibrating beats of my heart
And I'm engaged with the beauty of you as art
I feel this power over me like an intense drug
I'm stoned and high over my Rhythmic sense of Love

"Wow Terry, that was incredible. You did make that up right?"

"Yes I did and I have to say so myself, I like it!"

"Well Mr. Davis, I love it!"

"Ok where's mine Ms. Williams?"

"Terry, do I have to make one up too?"

"You bet your candy cakes my Dear!"

I couldn't wait to hear what Patrice can come up with and which subject she chooses to talk about, my guess will be that she talks about love.

"Ok Terry, I can talk about anything right?"

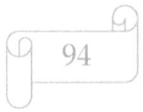

"Yes, feel free to talk about how sooooo handsome I am, just joking. Talk about anything Babygirl."

"Ok Terry, I'll name this one, *A Love Like Mine*."

"Ok Patrice, go ahead when you're ready."

A Love Like Mine
A love like mine
Touches and reaches you in time
Just in time, just as you needed
All the while you begged and pleaded
For something, someone, me
Asking how could this be
A love like mine, a torn heart like yours
No longer lonely like the empty shores
Instead, we're together for a lifetime
And you will be glad to have a love like mine

"Very nice Ms. Williams, very nice, so how would a love like yours be?"

"You will have to find out for yourself Mr. Davis."

"I plan to Ms. Williams."

"Stop making me blush Terry. I can't wait to see you later; ever since you left earlier I've been thinking about the next time I get to see you again."

"I can't stop making you blush, me making you blush is my way of moving the pain out of you and putting some love in you. And I can't wait to see you either!"

"Well Terry, it was lovely talking to you, but I'll let you go and I'll go finish and get ready for tonight, bye!"

"Ok babygirl, I'll talk to you later, bye!"

Chapter 17

Maria woke up from a mid-day nap that had produced some nightmares and deep sweats. She couldn't help but think about her next move of getting her Dr. T back. Also, she couldn't help but keep thinking about this Patrice lady that Dr. T screamed when she called.

Could he have possibly moved on to someone else? Like she really care, Dr. T was hers and she wasn't letting him go. Who could really pass up on all that she offered? Maria asked herself. She was "gorgiful Latino woman" as Dr. T put it.

Gorgiful was gorgeous and beautiful all tied into one. Maria was a strong woman, but couldn't't seem to find any one man enough to handle her. That was until she ran into her papi, Dr. T.

Maria walked into the bathroom and lit some candles so she could relax and think more about Dr. T. He was all the man she could ever ask for and that damn Daddy Dick just kept her pussy dripping wet all day. It was so big, so long, so thick and it always seemed to talk to her.

Her eyes were addicted to his six pack and her lips seemed to melt when they found his chest. Her hands dissolved when she rubbed them across his broad shoulders.

His eyes were a deep brown and Maria often found herself swimming in them and she tried not to look him dead in his bedroom eyes, but failed over, over and over again. She was brought out of her thoughts by a phone call that she hoped was Dr. T.

They were supposed to have a talk today and she didn't want to be the one to call him first. She wanted him to care enough to call her.

"What's up Chica?" Natalie screamed and instantly Maria let down.

"Hey Nat, what's going on mami?" She said with dull tone.

"Nothing girl, I'm just checking on you. You need to cheer up because I know you were expecting Dr. T."

"Whatever mami, I'm not even thinking about that man!"

"Yea right and I have a figure like Tyra Banks. Maria, it's me, I know how you're feeling. My question to you is, what are you going to do about it?" Natalie screamed into her ear.

"Well Nat, I'm seriously thinking about just showing up to his house and talking face to face with him, I think I have a better chance of hooking him that way, or at the very least, getting some of that Daddy Dick. There is a road block that I have ran across Nat."

"Aw shit girl, what is it now?" Natalie asked, already beginning to panic.

"I called Dr. T last night and he answered the phone screaming some woman's name."

"Damn Maria, that's fucked up for real. So again I ask, what yo' crazy ass gon' do girl?"

"Don't worry about it mami, trust me, I got this. Anyway, what's going on with you?" Maria asked, trying her best to change subjects.

"Well Maria, I do have some bad news. I got a call from my sister and my mom past away."
Maria sat in stunned in silence, for more than one reason. Natalie never talked about having a sister nor has she ever said one thing about her mother.

Maria thought about how selfish she had been. Natalie knew almost every aspect of what was going on with her and she never took the time to find out about her and her family. That made her realize how good of a friend Natalie had been to her and what a terrible friend she's been. Maria always had to tell my story and never really, sincerely asked about her until now.

"Nat, girl, I'm sorry to hear that. Are you ok? Is there anything I can do? I didn't even know you had a sister. That says how good of a friend I've been to you, huh?"

"Come on now Maria, don't worry about none of that. You know I ran away a long time ago and me and my sister hardly ever talk, so it's no big deal."

Maria had so many questions, but Natalie seemed ok about their relationship, where all they did was talk about Maria's issues. She seemed ok and took her mother's passing better than she'd ever seen anyone take losing their mom.

"So what did your mom die of?" She asked.

"Lung cancer. What are you going to do about Dr. T Maria?" Natalie asked, quickly changing the subject.

"Nat, do you not want to talk about this mami?"

"No, what are your plans now Maria?"

"Well mami, I think I am going to go over Dr. T's house and hopefully we can clear some things up and like I said, get me some of that Daddy Dick before I leave!"

"Well good luck with that. And stop worrying about me, I will be 'aight girl. Just make sure you call me later and let me know what happened. I'm going to call my sister and get the details on this funeral stuff."

"Ok mami, let me know if you need me for anything. I will definitely call you later, bye."

"Bye Maria."

Just like that, Natalie was gone and Maria was left there thinking about how she was going to go about going over Dr. T's house.

Maria walked around her house in nothing but her bra, panties and some heels. She wished her papi was there to bend her over and go to work.

Quickly but carefully, she did her makeup and then put on her black and silver Chanel dress that showed all of curves. She put in her platinum Chanel earrings to match. Maria did a little more touching up and then she was on her way to attempt to get her man back. As soon as she grabbed her keys and get ready to go, Dr. T called.

"Hello, this is Maria."

"Hi Maria, this is Dr. T. Are you busy?"

"No Papi, I'm just sitting here thinking about you and waiting for us to talk."

"Well Maria, there's really nothing for us to talk about except how things went on the phone last night."

"I know papi, what was that all about anyway and who is Patrice papi?"

"Look Maria, not that I have to explain anything to you right now, but Patrice is a friend of mine and some things happened last night and she was in need of my help, more like I tried my best to help her out and she is more than just a friend. I'm sorry Maria, but we just can't continue to talk. I don't believe it will be good for you or me."

Maria couldn't believe what she was hearing; it felt like someone was shoving a sword through her chest. Dr. T came off as if he had no love for her at all. He no longer cared how he said things to her. Maria became angry at Dr. T bluntness towards her.

"Papi…." Maria began to speak, but was interrupted.

"Maria, please stop calling me papi, I am Dr. T to you and really, I don't know if I'm that. You messed that up and I think we both can agree on that. Look I'm sorry if you think I am being evil, but covering up my true feelings right now will not do you any good."

"Dr. T, can I come by and see you?" Maria asked, totally dismissing what he told her.

"No Maria, you cannot come. Confusing things with sex is not the answer. Hell, all we ever had was sex. You lied to me when you had the chance to be honest, you had plenty chances to be honest and as a man who only tried to make you feel like a queen, you made me feel as if I failed over and over again. That can't be repaired. Look, I don't want to go into what all happened again, I just wanted to call and apologize for how I got off the phone with you last night. Even though you lied to me, I still wish the best for you and I wouldn't consider the option of intentionally hurting you."

"But Dr. T, you are what's best for me." Maria yelled, with tears filling her eyes.

"Maria, I am not the best for you. I'm sorry how everything has played out but it is what it is. I'm going to go now and I hope you find what you are looking for Maria and I wish you all the best. Good bye Maria."

After he hung up, Maria was left t here holding the phone up to her ear and tears ran down her face.

Even though she loved her some Dr. T, she was very pissed because he basically said what he had to say and didn't give a shit about hearing her out.

Maria could be the nicest, sweetest person in the world until you fuck her over and she definitely felt fucked over by Dr. T. He may think he's seen and heard the last of Maria, but little do he know, it's about to get real crazy, real soon.

She wanted to find out who this Patrice girl was because it may just get bad for her too. She didn't know the girl, but she was in her way and Maria was spoiled into getting whatever she wanted

Chapter 18

It was getting closer and closer to 8:00 pm. That's when Patrice was supposed to meet up with Terry and she couldn't wait. She felt her mom would just love Terry. He was sweet, nice and sensitive, but still very much a man.

Patrice tried so hard not to jump all over this man. He is gorgeous to her, his eyes are dreamy brown and her eyes soften at the sight of his skin. Terry had the cutest dimples she'd ever seen and every time he smiled, one side of his mouth curved a little higher than the other. When his succulent lips parted ways, they show his pretty white teeth.

She knew she would have to control herself tonight because the longer she was around him, the more she would want to give herself to him in a way she'd never given to a man.

Patrice continued to think about Terry while she packed some more of her moms things. She came across an old picture of herself when she was young.

It was her, her mom and dad and sister. Patrice never really told anyone that she had a sister because she abandoned them after their dad died. They would talk every couple of years, but there was no real relationship there. They didn't claim each other as sister, but Patrice felt she should at least call her and let her know about their mom.

"This is Natalie, who is this?"

"Uuumm hey Nat, it's me Patrice." Patrice spoke with a nervous tone, so nervous she felt her own voice tremble.

"Oh wassup?" Natalie said with what sounded like excitement.

"How are you?"

"I'm ok Patrice, what about you?"

"I guess I'm doing ok."

"Well girl, you don't sound like you're doing ok. Are you sure you're ok 'Trice?"

Natalie hadn't called her "Trice" in a long time and Patrice was caught off guard by it. She seemed like a different person, somewhat friendly.

"Natalie, are you ok? You seem different."

"How different?"

"Well it actually seems like you care."

"Some things changed 'Trice, I have a totally different outlook on things now. I only wish I had this outlook, years ago. How is everyone doing? How's mom doing?"

Patrice was still caught off guard by Natalie's attitude. She was expecting to tell her that their mom died and she would say ok and that would be it. She actually tried to hold a conversation with Patrice, which only made her job of telling Natalie about their mom that much harder.

"Well Nat, I have some bad news to tell you." Instantly, tears poured from her eyes.

"Trice, what's wrong?"

Natalie continued to try and figure out why Patrice was crying. Patrice found it difficult to break the news to her sister. No matter how hard she tried to control herself, the cries got louder and louder. She was still in disbelief that her mom was no longer here.

"Come on 'Trice, what's wrong? You're scaring me; please tell me what's wrong." Natalie begged.

"Nat, mom passed away early this morning."

There was silence on the other end of the phone.

"Are you bullshitin' me 'Trice? Are you just saying this to get me to come home, because if you are, that's fucked up!"

"No Nat, mom passed away early this morning. She died of lung cancer. I tried calling you a few months ago when we first found out about the cancer, but…you know?"

"Yea I know. I just hate I wasn't around while this was going on? I can imagine how stressful it must have been for you."

Natalie and Patrice went on and on about how they've been and how mom been. After all the crying, they actually started to act like real sisters.

"I'm sorry. I'm sorry for everything Trice. Do you want to get together later and talk about everything and maybe we can catch up?"

"Ok, seriously Nat, what's gotten into you? Why the different outlook, not that I don't like the change, I just want to know what caused it?" Natalie laughed on the phone while she sniffed.

"It's kinda embarrassing 'Trice."

"Well you gotta tell me then girl." They both laughed.

"Ok, a couple of weeks ago, I broke down to one of my best friends because I was so unhappy with the way I looked and the way I felt. I've gained a lot of weight since you last seen me 'Trice and I kept running into the wrong kind of guys. To make a long story short, she introduced me to this guy named Dr. T."

"He is the answer to all of our prayers. He knows what we want, how we want it and when we want it. Dr. T's main goal is to make sure all women know that they are queens and he makes us feel that way. Dr. T invited me over to his house one night and girl, he did some things to me that I never knew existed. Anyway, 'Trice, all I needed was that one time. That experience gave me so much confidence and it just changed how I view things. Dr. T told me to change the way I view things and things will change and he was so right about that."

"Well Nat, I'm glad you came across him because you seem totally different and that's a compliment!"

"So 'Trice, do you have a man? If not, I can give you the number to Dr. T and he can help you with anything?"

Patrice couldn't wait to brag about her Terry, even though officially nothing was official between the two.

"Naw Nat, I feel like I have my very own Dr. T. His name is Terry and you will like him because he treats me the same way Dad treated Mom. He opens my doors, puts my seat belts on for me. Terry does it all and he does it all without me hinting it to him. Terry also writes poetry and he can do it on the spot!"

"Shit, girl, Dr. T can do it on the spot too. And that Daddy Dick of his is amazing girl!" Patrice felt uncomfortable talking about sex and men right after she told her sister that their mom passed away earlier in the day. It was definitely unusual circumstances and Patrice was just happy to have her sister back and have girl talk. She was excited and felt her mom brought the two back together.

"Well I'm supposed to go see my Terry in a little bit."

"I hope you enjoy yourself and I'm glad we got a chance to talk, I only wish it was under different circumstances because I miss mom so much 'Trice. I can't wait to see you!"

"I can't wait either; we have a lot of catching up to do. I will talk to you later Nat, bye."

"Bye 'Trice."

Patrice was excited to have her sister back. She felt her mom, dad and God was up there making some things happen. On top of gaining her sister back, she had a great man, but she knew the devil was somewhere looking to mess it all up.

Chapter 19
Terry

Finally, I could start to prepare for my night with Patrice. I just got off the phone with Maria and I can admit I was probably a little rude or blunt, but like I told her, I had to say what I had to say and I had to say it the way that I did. Maria is known for always wanting to be in control and if I would have given her any hint that we could continue to see each other, she would've controlled the situation to get what she wanted.

I walked into the kitchen and poured me some Brandy and Coke until was no longer thinking about Maria, and all of my worries of her no longer existed. Tonight is all about Patrice. Although, I was a little worried because I haven't just enjoyed the company of another woman that I was interested in. Even though Dr. T had entertained many women, I never was interested in any of them.

I began to set the mood for romance by lighting some black love scented candles in every room. In the bathroom, I lit more candles and I ran bathwater with rose pedals floating on top. Taking in some more of my Brandy, I decided against romancing up the bathroom.

Dr. T kept trying to take control and I had to remember that this was not a sex date; this is me getting to know a beautiful woman that I am interested and just having a great time. I walked back into the kitchen to check on dinner that I was preparing for Patrice.

Since she mentioned to me that she loved soul food, I decided to make some pot roast with mashed

potatoes, greens and corn bread. Shit, I feel like eating right dayuum now. Suddenly my phone beeped as it alerted that I had a new text message. It read.

"Dr. T, thank you so much for our talk. But don't think this is over. I will catch you and your little bitch later!"

Shit, as if I already didn't have enough to think about. Now Maria wants to go and do this, and I could honestly say that I wasn't too surprised. I made another drink, this time minus the coke.

After a quick shower, I cut my hair and trimmed my goatee and sideburns so that it was even with my jaw line. I threw on one of my Jordan outfits. Not the Jordan athletic wear, but casual.

From the black button up shirt, black sports jacket, and denim jeans to the black Jordan dress shoes and finished the look off with some Giorgio Armani cologne. Now I was just waiting on my baby to get here.

I didn't concern myself with the text message, but I was seriously thinking of telling Patrice about this Dr. T thing. It may mess things up between me and her, but she has to know and I have to be the one to tell her.

It's still a mystery to me about how I was going to tell her about it, but something will have to come to mind. Just as I sat down, the door bell rang. It was Patrice.

"Hi Terry, did you miss me?"

"Ooooohhhh shiiit." I screamed and slammed the door right in her face.

"Terry, are you ok?" Patrice asked. I opened the door again.

"Yes babygirl, you just look so beautiful that I had to thank the Lord right away in private!"

Patrice had on a black and silver dress that was screaming for me just to take her. Take me Terry! Take me now, shit.

"There you go with that smooth talking again."

"Patrice, you were beautiful when I met you at Shania's and you were beautiful when we were at the

hospital, and now you are just stunning and I'm glad you're here me tonight."

Patrice was simply gorgeous. Her hair was long and wavy and her skin was flawless. Her lips glistened in a way that made me want to just blurt out '*I love you.*'

When she smiled, my world smiled. She walked like a woman who knew God and love had her back. Just on an act of instincts, I took her hand pulled her close to me. I stared into her eyes while stroking her face and slowly allowed our lips to meet each other.

I stood there kissing Patrice, tasting her lips while neither one us wanting to part ways. She wrapped her arms around me and I knew that while our wet lips continued to get wet, another part of her got moist also and right before she was about to explode and before I poked her to death, I pulled away.

"Wow, Terry you were right. Kissing you is like making love." Patrice said in a low mumble as she walked away.

Patrice asked for something to drink, so I made her and Brandy and Coke. I have to admit, I've never been so nervous around someone like I was around Patrice.

I tripped over something about three times already and it wasn't because of all the drinks I had prior. This woman does something to me without even knowing it. We settled down and talked for a while until the food was ready.

While she was talking to me, I tried my best to listen, but I couldn't help but think about the text message that Maria sent. Finally, we finished dinner and it was pretty quiet the whole time.

I cleared the table while Patrice made herself another drink and walked over to my brown leather sectional sofa. She motioned for me to put the dishes down and come join her. I followed her orders as *Nothing but Smooth Sailin*, by The Isley Brother's played in the background.

"Terry, have I ever told you I just love the way you walk? It's something about it that shows

confidence, power, and sensitivity. And I mean that in a very nice way."

I looked into Patrice's eyes without saying anything and slowly I massaged the palms of her hands with my fingertips.

"Thanks Patrice. I want to say I know it's only been a couple of days since we met and started talking, but I feel an amazing chemistry with you that I haven't felt for anyone in a very long time. And I just want to say I feel like the luckiest man in the world right now."

Patrice eyes slowly started to blink as she was being relaxed by the hand massage that I was giving her.

She sat up, pulled herself close to me so that we were literally an inch apart. She kissed me and instantly, I fell in love.

I could admit to myself that this was a scary feeling to have realized. A man like me couldn't fall in love. I mean can't and wanting to are two different things. I want to, I just can't.

Just like that, I thought about all the women that Dr. T had helped and the women that Dr. T would no longer be able to help. I started to feel that I would be letting down all women.

All I have ever told women was that they are queens and my only goal in life was to make sure that was possible. Now I'm sacrificing that for the happiness I longed for. One thing for sure, all the women may understand that I can no longer be Dr. T to them, except for Maria.

Me and Patrice kept kissing until she slowly pulled away, looking down then back up at me, she said "Terry, I have to tell you something."

Those were scary words to hear so suddenly like that. So I braced myself for whatever Patrice had to tell me.

"What is it babygirl?"

"Terry, I don't want to scare you off with what I'm about to tell you, but I want to be able to tell you any and everything and you should know some things about me."

Again, Patrice dropped her head and quickly I lifted it up by her chin.

"Babygirl, you can tell me anything. Remember that ok? Come on, look at me babe."

I kissed Patrice on the lips and tears started to slowly fall from her eyes as she looked at me.

"Terry, I'm not a virgin. Well I am, but I'm not. A couple of years after my dad died, my mom met this guy and just about every night he would touch me in places that he shouldn't touch me and he would come into to my room and do things to me that grown men shouldn't do to young teenagers."

"I lost my virginity to a man that my mom was supposed to be in love with. He begged me not to ever tell anyone or he would kill us all and finally after I felt I was already dead, I told my mom and she believed me. To make a long story short, he's now doing life in prison. I guess I wasn't the only little girl he was doing this to, but in the process my older sister moved out when she found out because she didn't believe nothing I said about that man because he and her grew a special bond together."

"I guess that was all part of his plan, but Momma believed me and that's all I needed."

Patrice dropped her head again and this time, I didn't take the time to lift her head back up because I was in total shock. First, I couldn't believe someone would do something like this. Secondly, Patrice never mentioned anything to me about a sister before and now I understand why.

"Patrice, I'm sorry to hear about all of this, I....I just...." Patrice interrupted.

"Terry, I don't want you to be sorry. I only told you this because.....because...." Patrice hesitated.

"Because what babygirl?" More tears fell from Patrice's eyes.

"Because Terry, I am in love with you and I want you to make love to me. I want to give you what no other man has deserved, my body and my love. I didn't intend on telling you that I love you, I didn't intend on telling you to make love to me Terry. All of this just happened, I mean, I knew that I was feeling

something for you, but it finally hit me I am in love."
Patrice was able to tell me her big secret and now was
the time that I have to tell her mine.

"Patrice, I'm glad you felt you could tell me
anything and now I must do the same. Before I start, I
have to say that I love you too......"

Before I could get another word out, Patrice
pounced on top of me. She kissed me with pure passion
and I enjoyed it heavily.

In no time, we were rolling around ripping each
other clothes off. For the first time, Patrice grabbed
hold of my dick and stroked it up and down. I rolled on
top of her and looked into her eyes and again, we kissed
passionately while she moaned '*make love to me
Terry.*'

I tasted a section of her neck and mde my
tongue go in circles in a spot that sent chills inside her.
Slowly I made my way down to her breasts while I
rubbed up and down her thighs. Slowly, I slid my hand
up her legs and pulled down her red lace thong.

I flicked my tongue to the beat of her heartbeat
on her nipples while I slid my fingers inside her sweet
underground. Patrice continued to moan while I feasted
upon her breast.

Slowly I moved down to her stomach and my
tongue traced a heart around her belly button. I made
my way down to her lucky charm that my fingers have
warmed up for me.

I kissed my way around her delectable garden so
I could build up the. She would be ready to explode the
exact moment my tongue tasted her.

Right before I tasted the juices that Patrice had
been marinating just for me, I pulled away and now I
was the one who dropped my head while dressing
Patrice up again.

She looked confused as she lay there begging
silently for some of what I started or at least an
explanation. I just couldn't do this until I knew Patrice
new the truth about me.

"Baby, what's wrong? Is it me? I knew I
shouldn't have told you that because now you're not
attracted to me."

Patrice couldn't be farther from the truth because I wanted her more than I've ever wanted anyone, but not like this, not until she knew. I've thought about just holding off on telling her, but I don't want to run the risk of her finding out from someone else or worse.

"Babygirl, this has nothing to do with you. I know I have fallen in love with you Patrice, but I just can't take this step with you until I tell you something about me."

"Ok, I'm waiting."

"Patrice, before we met, I was…I mean I…...."

"Just spit it out Terry." Patrice said as she sarcastically giggled

"Patrice, a few years ago I was hurt bad by a woman. I gave her everything in me, I did everything for her. I loved this woman harder than I even thought was possible, but she cheated on me plenty of times and I continued to take her back only because I believed I loved her. But the truth is, I believed in something so much, that I believed in it through the wrong person, an undeserving person. When we finally broke up or separated for good, she made me feel like I was responsible for it all and even though I knew I put my all into that relationship, she still made me believe that it was my entire fault. I was persuaded that I didn't know how to make her feel loved, I didn't treat her like a queen. All the things that women need to feel to know that they are loved; I felt that I did none of it. Patrice, I knew I did everything but it was stuck in my head that I could have always done more, and she wouldn't have felt the need to run to other men."

"Terry, if you were even an ounce of the man that I see right now, I'm sure that you were not the problem. She was just scared to walk away and be truthful to tell you that she wasn't interested anymore, so she cheated and made you feel that you were the reason. God sometimes brings people into our lives so lessons can be learned and then it's time for them to move on."

"I know all of that now Patrice, but I vowed that any woman that I saw, came across or was introduced

to, I would make them feel like queens. I put all my feelings to the side and my primary goal was to make a woman feel like a woman."

"And how would you do this Terry?" Patrice asked with some evilness in her eyes.

"Patrice, I would do it any way possible. If they needed to talk, they would come see me. If they need comforting, they would come see me and if they needed me to make love to them, I would....I'd... I would make love to them."

"Patrice, I had a gift. I knew what, when, where, how women wanted to be treated."

We both sat there in silence, me still with my head down and Patrice stared off into space trying to keep the tears from falling from her eyes.

"I had sex with these women, I made love to these women and I talked to them, gave them advice. Whatever they needed from me I was there. I was genuine in what I was doing. I wasn't just going around fucking anything that moved and I became this way because of how someone made me think. I hope you can believe me when I say that when I met you I stopped with everything. I built this alter ego and he was who everyone knew. You got to know Terry and Terry got to know you. The night after we met at Shania's, I cut it off with all the women I was involved with because I didn't want it to interfere with me and you. I did that well before me and you actually starting talking because I knew that I was very interested in you Patrice."

Patrice wiped her eyes and shook her head while mumbling to herself.

"Terry, please just answer one question for me."

"Yes Patrice, I'll answer any questions that you have."

"Are you Dr. T?"

"Shit!" How in the hell did Patrice know about Dr. T!

Immediately I started to think about Maria.

Instead of dropping my head, I lifted it up and looked Patrice right in her tearful eyes.

"Yes Patrice, I was Dr. T."

"I'm sorry Terry, but I have to go. I need some time to think about some things."

Patrice grabbed her things and headed for the door, and I pulled her to me and kissed her. She backed away with anger painted over her face.

"Is that how you kissed my sister Natalie?" Patrice walked away before I could answer. Now I'm left looking outside my door watching Patrice drive away, hopefully not driving away out of my life.

Chapter 20

Patrice finally made it home after a horrible night at Terry's that started off great. It seemed that they were going to have a very romantic night, but of course it seemed that way because as Patrice found out, he was accustomed to doing that kind of thing.

She couldn't understand, Terry was the perfect man. He made her feel special and wanted. When he touched her, her goose bumps fell in love and when he kissed her; her lips begged and cried out for more.

When Terry looked at Patrice, she melted. The man was just gorgeous and had the body of a God. She felt muscles on top of muscles and he had the cutest dimples that she's ever seen.

When he smiled, it was like nothing in her life was going wrong. She fell in love with this man, the only man that she's ever loved and he turned out to be the same man that slept with her sister.

Patrice flopped down next to some boxes that she packed up. She just laid there wondering what her next move would be.

The house just felt so empty. The disappeared sound of her mother's voice made her lonely. The sweet smell of breakfast in the mornings was no more and the banging of pots and pans came to a cease around dinner time.

It was even harder to handle now because before, she had Terry to help her cope. She also thought she had Natalie as well, but wasn't too sure after finding out the slept together.

Patrice had twelve missed calls on her phone and they were all from Terry. He left voicemails and sent some text messages, begging her to talk to him.

Deep down, she knew Terry didn't lie to her, but he slept with her sister.

She raised her self off of the boxes and leaned against her mother's favorite wooden rocking chair. She finally realized that Terry was the same man that Natalie claimed changed her whole attitude and just like that, she called Natalie.

"Hey girl, you back from your date already?"

"Natalie, how did you know it was me?"

"Shit girl, don't they have caller ID where you're from? I mean you did call from this number earlier." Natalie said while laughing.

"Yea, I'm just a little bit out of it right now. Natalie, I need a favor. I need you to tell me about Dr. T, everything you know!"

"Damn girl, was your date that bad?"

"Just tell me about Dr. T. What kind of guy is he?" Patrice asked, trying her best not to sound desperate.

"Well 'Trice, I will start off by saying that Dr. T will make some woman very happy when he decides to stop putting every woman before his own happiness. My only encounter with him was very special and I told you he gave me confidence that I never possessed. I'm a big girl and when he met me, girl he made me feel like I was a super model, Tyra Banks or some shit. When he touched me, he would........"

Patrice cut Natalie off because she still loved Terry and she couldn't hear about, in detail how he and her sister fucked.

"Natalie, what was his personality like? Did he just go around fucking people just for the hell of it?"

"Naw 'Trice. He was genuine with everything he did. If he told you something, he meant it and he proved it. Dr. T was a gift to us all and he helped me out and a lot of different other women. Personally I want him to find the right person and settle down because that's what he really wants. Deep down Dr. T wants the marriage and the kids, he doesn't want to be doing this shit forever even though it's a gift that he has. I think he's starting to realize that because he just cut off my best friend because she started to catch feelings with this nigga girl and he knew that he couldn't do his job if she felt that way and he didn't."

"My girl Maria is crazy, that's my best friend. She trying her best to get this nigga back and she think that he has moved on and found somebody that he is really interested in. Shit, she just got addicted to that Daddy Dick!"

Patrice almost dropped the phone because now there was more drama to the situation. First, he slept with her sister, and then he has a stalker that's her sister's best friend. Patrice was angry because she still loved this man.

"Natalie, I'm in love with Terry."

"Ok, girl good for you, but why are you asking about Dr. T then?"

"Natalie, Terry is Dr.T." They both sat on the phone in silence. Patrice went from leaning up against her mom's rocking chair to rocking in it.

"Trice, you bullshitting me right?" Natalie screamed.

"No Natalie, I'm not. I was over his house and we began kissing each other and just before we was about to make love, he stopped and told me this Dr. T shit."

"Yea, that's Dr.T. He wouldn't sleep with you unless he knew you knew the truth about him. Girl that means he care for you a lot. What nigga you know will stop right before fucking to tell you some shit like that. If anything, they would have waited until they got that nut first!"

As weird as Natalie put it, Patrice knew she had a point.

"So 'Trice, what did you say after he told you that?"

"Nothing, I just got my stuff and left. Terry has called, text, and left voicemails, but I haven't talked to him yet."

"Trice, if this was any other man, I would tell you to leave him alone, but Dr. T or Terry is different. Trust me."

"Natalie, what about your best friend?"

"Fuck her girl, you're my sister and she think she love him, but she only love that Daddy Dick, I'll handle that!"

Patrice's body cringed when she heard Natalie say Daddy Dick.

"Trice, go sleep on it and think about what I said. If you love Terry, you won't let him go."

"Ok, thanks Natalie. I'll go sleep on it and maybe talk to him tomorrow."

Patrice began to feel a little better about Terry. There was still Maria that could cause a problem though, but she loved her Terry and he loved her.

Chapter 21
Terry

What a night! What a fucking night! I thought I was doing a good thing by telling Patrice the truth and I still believed that it was the right thing to do, but damn.

I undressed to get ready for a shower. Maria kept texting me and every time I hoped it was Patrice. I called her, left voicemails, and text her, but she wouldn't respond to any of them.

While lifting my shirt above my head, I started thinking about what Patrice asked me. She asked me if I kissed her the same way I kissed her sister Natalie.

First, I had no idea that she had a sister and I definitely wouldn't have thought that it would be Natalie. I tried over and over again to call Patrice and Natalie, but I'm sure they were over there talking about me. I got another text message from Maria.

It would be best if you left that little bitch alone. I mean we wouldn't want any problems would we Dr. T? And if you don't think I'm serious, just try me. I know the bitch was at your house and I followed her ass home. She had on a cute dress by the way.

All I can do now is worry about the safety of Patrice. I knew how crazy Maria could get because she is used to getting what she wants and I'm what she wants.

I'm who she desired, but I could not and shall not give in to her desires. I am in love with Patrice and I will make her my wife one day.

Fresh out the shower, I threw on some basketball shorts and my Jordan flip flops. I end up having me another drink before I lay down to rest my head, but that may be awhile from now because Patrice is heavily on my mind.

I hope she was ok and a part of me wanted to drive over to her house just to make sure she was ok. Especially with me getting all these crazy text messages from Maria. Just as I was getting ready to sit down, my phone rang.

"Dr. mutha fuckin' T, what's up nigga?" JB screamed.

"Drama man, drama, what's up with you?"

"Just enjoying life brutha', so what's the drama about now?"

"JB a lot of shit just happened and I'm still shaking my head trying to figure it all out."

"What happened?"

"My baby Patrice came over and we had a nice talk. She was telling me some things that happened to her and her sister. Do you remember Natalie, Maria's friend that I slept with?"

"Yea man, the big girl? I still can't believe you hit that."

"JB, chill with that, anyway, Natalie ended up being Patrice's long forgotten about sister. So I guess Natalie told Patrice about Dr. T, not knowing me and Patrice were seeing each other. Patrice only knows me by Terry and Natalie only knows me by Dr. T. So with that, me and Patrice started kissing and shit, then my ass pulled up and stopped everything." JB blurted out laughing. JB was my best friend, but sometimes he can be a straight up asshole.

"Nigga, why the hell did you stop? You should have at least got that nut first!"

"It's not about that with Patrice. JB, I need you to be serious because I have a lot of shit going on!"

"Ok man, my fault." Just like that, JB's tone changed.

"Like I was saying, I stopped everything and told her about Dr. T."

"How did she take it?" JB asked with concern in his voice.

"Honestly JB, I think she would have taken it better if I hadn't slept with her sister, but it's not like I knew they were sisters, hell I didn't even know Patrice when me and Natalie slept together. JB, that's not it either. Now Maria is acting crazy as shit!"

"Nigga, I thought you let her go?"

"Shit I did, but we talking about Maria. She's sending crazy ass messages threatening Patrice."

"Dayuum Terry, this is some serious shit. What you gon' do?"

"I was thinking about driving over Patrice's house just to make sure she's ok because Maria sent a message saying that she followed her home. Yea man I know Patrice is upset with me, but I'm about to get ready to go over there."

"Terry be careful out there. I know I joked around before saying that you and Maria were meant to be together, but she seems crazy for real. Do you need me to ride with you?"

"Naw JB, I can handle Maria. I'm getting another text message from her."

"Shit Terry, what does it say?"

"Fuck!!! She's right outside Patrice's window, looking at her right damn now! JB if you don't talk to me tonight or tomorrow morning, call these numbers. I have to go man; I'll get at you later!"

JB tried his best to ask me something, but I had already hung up the phone. I gave him Natalie and Patrice's phone numbers just in case something happened. I threw on some clothes and left the house to go make sure my baby was ok.

Chapter 22

As I walked out the door, I got a text message from Maria asking me if I would marry her. What the hell was wrong with her? Finally, I decided to stop with all this text message shit and gave her a call because I couldn't continue doing this. It had to end at some point and I would be the one to put it to an end.

"Hey papi, so what's your answer to my proposal?"

"Maria, what the hell is your problem? I tried to be nice and let this go away easy, you need to do the same."

"Papi, you're just tired. You always had a short temper when were tired."

"Maria, stop calling me papi. I'm not your fucking papi so stop calling me that."

"Dr. T if you know what's best for you and your little bitch, you would agree that you are my papi because I'm looking dead at her and she doesn't seem to know that I'm pointing something long and shiny right at her. Dr. T you are making this a lot harder than it really has to be."

"Maria, I'm not Dr. T anymore, my name is Terry. You always asked me, how long was I going to be doing this Dr. T thing and when was I going to settle down and have a family. Well I found someone that I want to settle down with."

"Well Terry, or whatever your name is, what do your little bitch think about Dr. T?"

"Maria, what do you want from me?" I asked in a tone that let her know I was tired of all the games that was being played.

"Daddy Dick, I want Daddy Dick. I have to admit it Terry, you have a nice package on you and I just have to know that your package will always be handled by me!"

"No Maria, I can't do that. I'm no longer Dr. T; I no longer have the mindset to make every woman feel like queens. I just want to make one special lady feel like she's a queen." I'm sure Maria could sense the frustration building in my voice.

"That's good papi, because I can be your queen."

"No you can't. I'm in love with someone else Maria, deal with it!"

"Ok Terry, since you mentioned deal, let's make a deal. How about you still give me my Daddy Dick whenever I want it and you can still have your little bitch on the side."

It burned me up inside hearing Maria call Patrice a bitch, it took me to a place where I didn't need to be. I wanted to hurt Maria; I wanted to hurt Maria bad. I wanted her out of my life for good, but I knew I couldn't do what I really wanted to do.

"No Maria, I can't do that and you know I can't do that."

"Ok Terry, I'm just going to spell it out for you just like this. You are going to be with me or something terribly bad is going to happen to this little bitch that you want to be with. I don't see what you see in her anyway. I look way better than her, besides I want you for myself. I'm sorry I had to lie to you before papi, but I just tried to cover up my feelings until one day, I just couldn't do it anymore. I had to tell you how I felt."

"You're right Maria, you lied to me and that's when I had to cut you off. Patrice never lied to me. You can try and bully your way into getting what you want, but I swear to God if you hurt Patrice, I will......."

"You will do what papi? What would you do to the woman you love papi?" Maria interrupted.

"Look, I told you to stop calling me papi, or Dr. T. If you hurt Patrice, I will kill you!"

"Terry, I love you!"

"Maria, no you don't!"

Maria was in love with the idea of being in love. One thing was for sure, she loved Daddy Dick. Her pussy did cuff my dick just right, but it's not about that. Could I have possibly been with Maria in the way that she wants? Probably could because Maria had a sexy body and she's smart, but when I first met Maria, she told me that she was married and she just wasn't happy. She lied about it all and ever since she confessed to me about lying, I hadn't wanted anything to do with her and it will remain that way.

Maria and I went back and forth on the phone and the whole time, I prayed that Patrice was doing ok. Maria finally started to calm down and the tone in her voice was more of hurt. Which I could understand, but that was no longer my problem. She caused all of this by lying to me.

"Terry, you have to know that I love you and I don't want to be with anyone else. You always made me feel good and not only when we fucked either. I just thought me and you were building something special with what we had going on."

"Maria, I'm sorry that you thought that, but I always made sure you knew that it was nothing more than what it was. I wanted you to feel like a queen when you went home to your husband and for a while you told me that it was working. You felt like a queen all the time around your husband. So can you blame me for doing what I did because you lied to me?"

"Ok Terry, I'm tired of talking, so you need to answer the question that I asked you."

"What question is that Maria?"

"Will you marry me?"

"No!" I yelled.

"Fine have it your way, but you don't have to worry about Patrice, because although I did follow her home, that's not where I am."

"Well where are you Maria?"

"You will find out soon, Goodbye Terry."

Just like that, Maria hung up the phone. I looked down at my phone to make sure she hung up and glanced back at the road to see Maria driving head on towards me.

Other than seeing my airbag and the shattering of glass, I didn't know what happened or where I was, but I definitely, definitely know something wasn't right.

Chapter 23

The long night was finally over for Patrice. She woke up and laid in her bed wishing Terry didn't tell her what he told her. She wanted to be in his arms right now on this beautiful morning.

She remembered her mother would lie in the bed just the way she was doing, but wondered what kind of thoughts she had.

Patrice rolled over and clenched onto one of her pillows, thinking, wondering about what she was going to do. She hadn't received any more text messages or calls from Terry since last night and in a way, she felt bad for him. He tried to do the right thing by telling her the truth, but Patrice didn't think she could get over him doing that kind of thing, especially to her sister.

She battled with the fact that Terry didn't know they were sisters. Not only that, he didn't even know she had a sister. Natalie felt that Patrice should sleep on it and then decide what she wanted to do. She didn't feel any better about it even though Natalie had nothing but good things to say about Terry or Dr. T.

Natalie didn't know Terry, she only knew Dr. T, but she still spoke highly of him. Patrice wasn't sure what to do so she decided to call Terry, but her calls and text went unanswered. The more she called, the more she got worried and concerned.

Terry wasn't the man to ignore her calls or text. Even if he knew she was upset with him, he would still answer her calls. A couple of hours had past and still no call from Terry. She knew he liked to drink his Brandy whenever he had a lot of stuff going on. Patrice began to panic, so she called Natalie to see if she heard anything.

"What's up girl?" Natalie answered sluggishly.

"I'm sorry to wake you up Natalie, but I'm starting to get a little bit worried about Terry." Still half asleep, Natalie replied.

"Who?"

"Natalie get up! I think something is wrong with Terry!"

"Girl, what are you talking about? I thought you didn't want to talk to him anyway?"

Natalie was, Patrice didn't want to talk to him anymore, but she wasn't sure about her decision. She was more worried than anything else.

"I didn't, but he stopped calling me and not taking my calls. That's not like Terry at all to do something like that."

"Ok 'Trice, when was the last time you actually talked to him?"

"Shit, when I confronted him about being Dr. T."

Patrice felt horrible about it because Terry actually tried telling her the truth.

"Natalie, I don't know what I would do if something happened to him. I was in love with him and he's the first man besides dad that told me he loved me."

"Patrice, you just need to calm down girl. You know he likes to have a couple drinks when he has a lot on his mind. I'm sure he just had too much to drink last night and he's knocked out over there."

Patrice was able to calm down a little bit, but she knew her Terry. She knew that he would still answer his phone. While she listened to Natalie go on and on about Terry being ok, a number buzzed in on her phone that she didn't recognize. Patrice hoped and prayed that it was Terry calling her. She clicked over without letting Natalie know.

"Hello? Terry, is that you?"

"Hi, may I speak to Patrice please?"

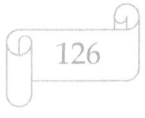

Immediately she was disappointed that Terry's voice is not on the other end of the phone.

"This is Patrice. Who is this?"

"Hi Patrice, my name is James, James Billings and I am Terry's best friend. He gave me your number and Natalie's number last night before he left. Terry told me that if I haven't heard from him by this morning, I should give you a call. Have you heard from him?"

"No I haven't. What are you talking about? What happened last night that he felt he had to give you our numbers?"

Patrice wasn't sure if she should believe this man or not. She decided to buzz Natalie in on their conversation. She was still oblivious to the fact that Patrice got off the phone.

"James, I have Natalie holding on the other line, so I'm going to bring her in ok?"

"Ok Patrice, that's fine."

"Hey Natalie, I have this guy on the other line that says he is Terry's best friend, I'm going to bring you in on three way."

"Ok 'Trice."

"James, I'm back on Natalie is on here too. What happened last night that he felt he needed to give you our phone numbers?"

"Terry gave them to me. I need to know if either of you has heard from Terry this morning?"

Both, Patrice and Natalie replied no at the same time with concern now coming through their voices.

"James, neither one of us has heard from Terry, so can you please just tell us what happened because y'all woke me up out my sleep for this shit?" Natalie said.

"I'm sorry to have to be the one to call you with this, but I think something may have happened to Terry. Last night he called me after you left Patrice. He was upset because he felt he was doing the right thing by telling you the truth, but anyway, he kept getting these text messages from a lady that's been stalking Dr. T. He stopped talking to this lady, for one, she lied to him and second, he fell in love with you Patrice."

"Wait.....just wait one dayuum minute." Natalie said as she interrupted James.

"James, is the bitch named Maria?"

"Nat, who is Maria?" Patrice asked, feeling left out of the loop.

"That's my best friend. Shit, the one I told you introduced me to Dr. T. She told me that she wasn't going to let anybody have Dr. T, but I didn't think the bitch was crazy enough to do something to him!"
"I still can't believe I'm still in love with him knowing he has a crazy stalker after him." Patrice said.

"Patrice, it's not even like that. Shit, I just found out that Terry and Dr. T was the same damn person, besides, I told you about Maria a few minutes ago, girl you need to calm down."

"This is getting too deep for me." Patrice said, becoming more and more angry.

"Ladies, I know all about both of you, also Maria. Like I was saying, he called me to talk about his night with Patrice and Maria kept texting him shit all through the night and even after you left Patrice. She sent him a text message saying that she saw you leave his house, so she followed you home and was looking at you through your window. She threatened to do something bad to you. That's when he left to come and check on you Patrice. That's why he gave me you ladies number. Terry said if I didn't hear from him by this morning, I should call you both."

"I'm going to kill that bitch." Natalie screamed. Patrice couldn't blame her, but she wanted to be one that took care of Maria. She was still unsure if she could accept that Terry had this Dr. T shit going on. She did know that he was trying to do the right thing and he didn't deserve this, if something did happen to him. All she could think about was that Terry was trying to save her, even though she ran out on him.

"I think we should call the police and check all the hospitals to see if Terry is at any one of them." James suggested.

Natalie and Patrice both thanked James for calling and they all got off the phone with their instructions on whose calling what and where.

Tears fell from Patrice's eyes as she couldn't believe what was really going on.

She met this great man at Shania's, she lost her mom, fell in love with a man, reunited with her sister, found something out horrible about the man she loved and now she may have to come to terms of losing him. Patrice wondered if love was really worth all of this.

She asked herself repeatedly if she could let it all go and find someone else to fall in love with. She sat in her mom's favorite rocking chair again and watched the news to collect her thoughts and finally, someone else had some drama going on.

Patrice sipped her coffee and then leaned forward to hear what was happening on the TV. Apparently there was a bad accident last night and they had to rush some lady to the hospital. Patrice jumped and spilled coffee spills as she saw Terry being carried to a helicopter and air lifted to the hospital.

Chapter 24
Momma and Pappa Davis

Where in the hell am I at? The last thing I remember was seeing Maria come head on, aiming right for me. The only conclusion I can draw was that I died and I'm in heaven right now.

I must say that my visions of heaven were nowhere near close to the real thing. I was expecting some shiny bright light and I thought I would meet Jesus before I was let into the gates. It seemed peaceful up here, but of course it does, it's Heaven.

There were children playing in the green grass that hinted nothing short of happiness and the air was as fresh as to be expected and brought new meaning to the phrase '*a breath of fresh air*.' The elderly men sat and conversed about the times they had on earth and the elderly women knitted with smiles across their faces.

It was almost as if I was gliding through heaven because I didn't feel myself walking, but I was definitely moving. Everyone had smiles painted on them and you could tell that there was no such thing as worries up here. One old lady came up to me and just hugged me and kept walking.

She looked very familiar and as she walked off, I realized that it was Patrice's mom. I watched her for awhile as I saw her grab hold to a man's hand. I was sure it was Patrice's father, because she looked just like him. I took a seat on this old wooden bench and sat there to collect my thoughts. I began thinking about Patrice and instantly, I, a grown man, was brought to tears. I was in love with this woman. It's funny how your past and present doesn't let you know that you will regret what you're currently doing in your future. Even if you believe that what you're doing is the right thing.

I was having sex, or making love to all these women, genuinely because I wanted to give them a piece of life that they lacked. Sex isn't just sex and love isn't just love. It's a connection, a feeling, an emotion and I had the gift to give that to women and make them feel like queens in the process. For that, I sacrificed my chance of falling in love and having a connection, a feeling or an emotional connection with a woman I wanted for myself.

I fell in love with Patrice for only a short while, but that short while was better than anything I had ever experienced before and now it's taken away from me. I could only imagine what Patrice is thinking right now. I'm sure she's not too happy with God right now, being that she feels He took her mom away from her and now I've been taken away from her.

I sat on the wooden bench with my head buried in my hands and just like that, I got chills when I heard the most pleasant voice in the world.

"Baby, what's wrong?"

Tears steady flowed as I raised my head up to see a beautiful woman in a flower dress and I knew without seeing her face that is was Momma. I was back a little boy, crying in my momma's arms as she held me. It's amazing how she could hold me and still make everything seem ok. She encouraged me to cry.

"Get it all out baby. Yea, there you go baby." She would say.

Then my dad walked up and a smile came over my face because I realized where I got my walk from. Dad had a look of mixed emotions painted on his face. I could tell that he was happy to see me, but a look of concerned was also dressed on his face.

Momma continued to look at me while she rubbed my hands. Her smile never vanished from her face and her touch was still a touch of grace. She had long, peppered hair and her skin was flawless. I had my mother's smile and eyes.

My dad stood tall above us while we sat on the old crackling bench. His huge hands covered the curve of momma's shoulders and his eyes covered me like an eclipse. Daddy knew why I was there and he was not too happy about it.

I was blessed with my dad's jaw line and high cheek bones, so it was very easy to tell when he was not happy about something. He spoke not often, but that made his words that much more important when he did have something to say.

Momma let go of my hand and grabbed dad's, as if to say, calm down.

"Baby, your father and I are not too happy to see you here. We watch over you all the time and we both knew this day was coming. Now baby, I know everything about what you have been doing and I'm glad to see that you are ready to change. You are ready to change aintcha?" Momma asked.

I could tell she was about to start grilling me, but she still kept a smile on her face.

"Yes momma, I think I found the one I really want to be with, but I have come across some struggles in getting the necessary people out of my life."

"I tell ya one thing, it's not gon' be over with for a while. So baby if you really loved this girl, you should of made sure that you ended it right with that trouble maker. Baby I will tell you that if you do everything that you're supposed to do, you will get exactly what you're looking for and more with this new lady that you claim you love. She seems pure and genuine and that's the kind of lady my baby needs in his life. You need to rid yourself of all that you are doing because it's damaging you and keeping you from the blessing that God has in store for you baby."

Momma went on and on about me needing to make sure it was over. The way she spoke, was as if I have another chance at this thing, but I'm dead. There will be no more chances. I figured Maria survived the accident because I have yet to see her up here or maybe she didn't make it and she just got invited to Hell instead. Momma tried desperately to address the whole Dr. T issue, but thankfully dad stepped in.

"Come on baby, I'm sure Terry knows everything that he's done wrong. Right now is not the time to go over everything that he's done wrong. Son, I want you to know that I'm proud of you. You may not remember, but when you were little, I use to always come and talk to you while you were in your crib. I use to preach to you how important it was to make your lady and any lady feel like princesses and queens. I think you did a great job at that son. What I didn't tell you that I should have, is that some women are incapable of knowing what real love is. Sometimes, it is to no fault of their own, but not only men, but life, their parents or different events in their lives damaged them so much that they do not recognize when someone truly loves them. They put up this wall that their hearts won't let them take down. You were damaged too son. You let a woman tell you something about yourself that you knew wasn't true. You knew that it was far from the truth, but instead you didn't realize your own worth. You listened to her and created someone that has helped a lot of women, but also done more damage to you than good."

Dad stood over mom lecturing me, but praising me at the same time. Mom still had that gorgeous smile on her face and an everlasting twinkle in her eye. My dad definitely had a point.

Dr. T was doing something good for these ladies, but was damaging me in the process. I wasn't the creator of Dr. T. The damage that this woman did to me was the creator and I was just the manager of him. Out of nowhere, momma hugged me and started crying and even dad had a tear in his eye.

"Momma, why are you and Daddy crying?"

"Because we see our baby is hurting and we can't do anything about it. We left you when you were only three years old baby that was nowhere near enough time to prepare you for the world. That was our main goal when we brought you into this world."

Momma continued to talk and cry at the same time, but while she talked, my vision got very blurry. My eyes opened and closed in slow motion and everything around me slowly started to fade to a sight of blackness. I can still hear momma talking.

"Baby, are you ok?"

"Son, can you hear us?" My dad asked.

"Son it will be ok, it's time for you to leave us. God is not ready for you yet. We will always be here for you son."

I was no longer able to hear what my mom and dad was saying. I wasn't able to neither hear nor see. I just saw darkness. Close your eyes and tell me what you see.

That exactly what I see… Darkness…

Chapter 25

Patrice finally made it to Henderson Methodist Hospital and it brought back the same feelings she had when she watched her mom pass away.

The hospital smelled the same and she nearly fainted as soon as she stepped foot in the emergency room. She called Natalie and James as soon as she saw Terry on the news.

She immediately ran to the front desk in a frantic sprint. It was only fitting that Patrice had to get a ghetto chick to assist her at the front desk. She had loud colored fingernail polish and purple hair and her name tag read, Shemetriantey.

"Excuse me ma'am, I need to know which room Terry Davis is in?"

"Name?"

"I told you it was Terry Davis!"

"Naw girl, what's yo' name?" Shemetriantey asked as she smacked her lips.

"My name is Patrice."

"Can you sign in please?"

Patrice wanted so badly to ask her why did she ask her name if she was just going to sign in.

"Here you go ma'am."

"Y'all relatives?" Shemetriantey asked.

"Excuse me lady, that's my man in there so can you please just give me the dayuum room number!?"

Shemetriantey curled her lips, raised one finger up and looked Patrice up and down. She smacked her blue lipsticked lips at Patriced and said "You ain't got to get no attitude. He down the hall in room 482.

Visiting hours are over tho', but you can wait for him in the waiting area and the doctors will come out and talk to you."

Patrice didn't stay to finish hearing what the loud woman had to say. She sprinted down to where she saw a doctor standing.

"Excuse me doctor, are you working on Terry Davis? How is he? What's wrong with him? Is he going to make it?"

Patrice had question after question and didn't stop to take a breath in between questions. She felt somewhat guilty for what happened to Terry and wanted to make sure she did everything she could to find out he was ok. She felt if she had just stayed there and listened to Terry, none of this would have happened.

"Just calm down Ms.?"

"Williams."

"Just calm down Ms. Williams, I will be working on Mr. Davis and as soon as I know what's going on, I will come out here and keep you updated."

This doctor tried his best to calm Patrice down, which was impossible because he still hadn't gave her any information on Terry.

He walked into the room, leaving her there to wait in the waiting room alone at 2:15 in the morning.

The halls were dark and dim even though the lights were still on.

There was a smell of medicine everywhere around her and she kept seeing nurses walk by. Patrice buried her head in her hands and prayed to God that Terry would be ok. She was already afraid and anticipating something bad to happen because she had bad luck with this hospital and didn't get a good feeling.

Tears kept pouring from Patrice as she continued to be in disbelief what she was being faced with.

She raised up and wiped her eyes when she heard Natalie down the hall arguing with Shemetriantey. Patrice jumped out of her seat and signaled for Natalie to come over.

"Have you heard anything from the doctors yet?" Natalie asked hurriedly and out of breath.

"Not yet. The doctor said that he will be out to talk to me as soon as he knows something. Natalie, have you talked to Maria yet, has she called you?"

Patrice knew Maria was Natalie's best friend or was her best friend and she so badly wanted to find out where she was. She daydreamed about what she would do the moment she saw Patrice.

"Naw 'Trice, I haven't heard from her. If the accident was as bad as you say it looked on the news, then I'm sure her crazy ass up in here too and I can't wait to find her."

Natalie and Patrice went back and forth talking about what they were going to do to Maria if they ever got their hands on her. A dark, tall and skinny man walked up and stood directly in front of the two women.

"Excuse me, can I help you?" Natalie asked.

"Yes, by any chance are you Natalie and Patrice? I'm James."

"Yes, I'm sorry about that. I'm Natalie and this is my sister Patrice." Natalie said, apologizing for her rude greeting.

"Hi ladies, it's nice to finally meet you. Terry has told me a lot about you, especially you Patrice. Have you heard anything from the doctors?"

"No, they haven't come out yet." Patrice explained while wiping her cried out eyes. On cue, the doctor came out of Terry's room. He approached the three while he's taking off his gloves. Patrice rushed up to the doctor and bomb rush him with questions.

"How is he doing doctor?" She asked, with a look that begged for good news.

"Well Ms. Williams, it seems that Terry has suffered some head trauma. I have some good news and not so good news. We tried to get him to respond to us, but it was to no success. He is breathing fine and has a normal blood pressure. The bad news is that he is showing all signs of being in a coma."

Patrice saw James and he had his head down. She then glanced at Natalie and they both started crying uncontrollably.

Somehow, someway, questions still were able to come out of Patrice's mouth.

"Doctor, what exactly does a coma mean? All I know is that he is in a deep sleep and you never know how long it could last. What symptoms does he have that lets you know he is in a coma?"

"First off, you can call me Dr. Wolciek. Terry is experiencing some swelling in his brain and right now we will have to keep a very close eye on him. We will do a full set of laboratory test. We will also do a plethora of blood test that checks the liver, kidney and thyroid function, glucose levels and the presence of any toxins. The result of these tests will give us clues as to what caused the coma."

"Also, I will examine his eyes using a fundoscope. A fundoscope is used to examine the optic nerve in the back of the eye for any signs of swelling which tells us that there could be increased intracranial pressure."

Patrice stood motionless in front of the doctor, frozen in movement. She couldn't believe that the man she loved was in a coma.

"How long will he be in a coma?"

"Well Ms. Williams there is no set time that we can tell you. It can last for a couple days, months, or even years. I do want to make you aware Ms. Williams that there is a possibility Mr. Davis could wake up with some memory loss. It doesn't happen to all comatose patients, but I just wanted to give you that information so you won't be shocked if that is the case."

Natalie put her arms around Patrice to console her. Patrice buried her head on Natalie's chest and continued to cry and wonder why all of this happened to her.

The entire time the doctor was talking, James had his head down, but he finally raised it up and asked a question in a strong but soft spoken voice.

"Excuse me Dr. Wolciek, but do you know anything about how this happened to Terry?"

"All I know is that it was a very bad accident and there seem to be some indication that this was done to him intentionally. The police are still investigating the case. That's about all I can share with you and I really wasn't supposed to share that little bit of information."

James turned his head and walked away mumbling to himself.

"Do you know if the person that hit him is here?" Natalie asked.

"Again, I can't share anymore information unless it's about Terry's condition."

James punched a wall behind the girls and it got the attention of security.

"Ms. Williams, I have to go back in and check up on Terry. If there is any news, I will contact you.

Does Terry have any family that we need to notify?"

"Dr. Wolciek, we are the only family that Terry has. You can contact me anytime." Patrice explained with a blank look on her face and slow crackling in my voice.

Dr. Wolciek said Patrice would be the one he contacts with any information regarding Terry and suggested the all went home for the night.

Patrice tried to make her way back there to see Terry, but they wouldn't allow her to. She walked back over to the waiting area with her arms folded and a hunch in my back. She walked slow and steady while praying all the way to her seat.

She prayed that Terry would somehow make it out of this situation because he didn't deserve it.

James and Natalie insisted she go home for the night, but Patrice was in no way in the right frame of mind to drive home. Plus, she wanted to be there early in the morning to check on Terry.

James went from being a cool soft spoken guy to being very pissed off and cursing to himself. He managed to calm himself down enough to go give Patrice a big hug before he left. She knew then, that he was really the best friend of her Terry.

Natalie begged and pleaded for Patrice to go home, she even volunteered to drive her home, but she wasn't going anywhere.

The two ladies watched James walk off and they talked a little more.

Patrice finally told her sister that this was the hospital their mom died at and Natalie started crying all over again.

She apologized once again for not being there all those years and especially when mom died. Natalie promised that she will always be there for Patrice from now on. Before she left, she had to go start another argument with Shemetriantey, but she came back with a blanket and laid it over Patrice. She kissed her on her cheek and walked off.

Chapter 26

Two weeks have gone by and there was no improvement from Terry. Patrice has been at the hospital everyday hoping and praying for a miracle that one day Terry will at least open his eyes. In a way, she wanted her face to be the first thing he see upon awakening.

Every visit to Terry was the same, she couldn't help but break down and start crying because she didn't know what's going to happen with him. She imagined how much pain he must of felt. The corners of Patrice's mouth erected in a smile while envisioning him saying *'come on babygirl, stop all that crying.'*

He was the love of her life and even though she's been here for Terry every single day, she still had her own things to battle with. Did she want to put all of her trust in a man that slept with her sister and who knows how many other women?

Patrice kept hearing nothing but good things about this man from everyone involved, but it was still hard. She wondered what thoughts would cross her mind every minute he was away from her. Could she trust him enough not to worry about that?

She sat next to Terry, holding his hand and it was so hard for her to see him like this. He had tubes up his nose and wires attached to his head and chest. The heart monitor kept beeping, but all she could think was that the machine is counting down the time until it's no longer beeping and her Terry would be taken away from her.

"Terry baby, I know you can't hear me, but I just wanted to let you know I love you and I'm sorry that this has happened to you. The police are investigating what happened that night and I suggested to them that they check your phone records and then they would realize that this was done intentionally to you. They would know that Maria was behind all of this."

Patrice wiped her tears away and began to smile at some of the memories they shared. She realized she didn't have to talk to him about the investigation at that moment. In a half laugh, half cry, she started to share with Terry some good times that they had.

"Terry, do you remember when we first met? I remember sitting down doing some writing and the next thing I know, a tall, handsome man walks up to me smelling all good. I could tell you were nervous. You just had a look in your eye that said, '*shit I'm nervous.*' I saw you walking up to me and I couldn't help but fall for your walk. Although you were nervous, your walk wasn't. It screamed out confidence. Terry, it wasn't how you looked that had me interested in you, it wasn't even the swagger that your walk possessed. It was how you talked to me; you were soft spoken but still strong and confident in what you were saying. I remember you saying I will always get what's meant to be said and not what's thought about. You said what you wanted to say and you didn't care whether it was corny or not. Shania's, that was our spot, that's were all of this started. Then sadly, our next encounter was at this very hospital. You were so gentle with me, yet so strong. You held me the way I wanted and needed to be held. You touched me like I was the only thing in the world that existed. You talked to me like I was the only person that mattered and the way you looked at me, it made me feel like you looked me directly in my eyes and you found my heart somehow."

Patrice grabbed hold to both of Terry's hands and laid her head on his chest. It was amazing that he was the one lying in a hospital bed, in a coma and yet he still comforted.

Just lying there made everything better for that moment. For that point in time, her tears went away and her worries were a little less now.

As soon as Patrice lifted her head off Terry's chest, she heard a slow moan from Terry and she couldn't have jumped out her chair fast enough to go and tell the doctors. They quickly followed the excited Patrice back into the room, but then they asked her to leave and wait outside.

She's been there for Terry every day since the accident and there was no way she was leaving that room. All of the doctors and nurses knew me and they knew she was all Terry had, but they insisted that it would be better if she allowed them to do their job.

Patrice figured that they needed to do what they needed to do without her in there to make it better for Terry, so she waited and waited outside the room while they worked on Terry.

"Ms. Williams?" Patrice was awakened by Dr. Wolciek hours later.

"Yes?" She responded with her eyes barely open and her hair everywhere.

"Again, I have some good news and some not so good news about Terry."

"Ok Dr. Wolciek, give me the bad news first."

She always wanted to hear the bad news first so she could determine for herself if it was really bad news.

"Well remember when I cautioned you that Terry may have some memory loss?"

"Yea."

"Well there's a strong possibility that he may have some memory loss. The good news is that by looking at some of his brain activity, it doesn't look like it will be permanent so if you're up to it, you may have a task on your hands getting him to remember certain things. The other good news is that Terry is no longer in a deep coma. He is in what we call a vegetative state. That is where he may make sounds, cry, or smile. He could even begin to open his eyes and move them toward people or objects. Being in a vegetative state, means that he could return from a wake-sleep cycle and he could possibly react to sounds also. Other things to know is that Terry will have no purposeful movements nor will he be able to follow any directions and don't expect him to have any forms of communication with you right now. There is no time line for how long he could be in a vegetative state. Now, usually a patient can be released for home care while they are in a vegetative state, but I recommend keeping Terry here since he has no actual family."

Patrice couldn't believe what she was hearing. None of that was good news to her, but she figured the only good news she wanted was hearing Terry is back to normal and he can leave today with no lingering issues.

She went back and forth in her mind debating whether or not to keep Terry here or take him to her house, but she realized that it may be better for him to stay there at the hospital. Patrice knew they would give her instructions on how to care for Terry, she just felt it best for him to stay around some doctors and she told Dr. Wolciek that very thing.

She asked how Terry was doing and Dr. Wolciek said that he was doing about the same and suggested that she go home and get some rest.

Chapter 27

It's been a wild couple of weeks with everything that's happened and Natalie didn't see any signs of it slowing down. She still worried about Patrice and Terry. Even thought its been a few weeks, Natalie was still emotional from her mother's funeral. After all the time away from her, she still looked the same and Natalie just wished she could take it all back.

She called Patrice that morning when she woke up, but her calls went unanswered. Natalie knew she was dealing with Terry and she hoped everything was better for them.

She walked over to her black leather couch to get me some relax time in before her day started. Just as she got comfortable, she saw that Maria was calling.

Parts of her didn't think she was ready to answer that call, but the majority part of her was saying, '*Bitch, what the fuck are you waiting on.*'

She had to play it cool because Maria was still her best friend and she didn't want her to know that she knew what was going on. Natalie knew she couldn't just off on her the way she wanted to. Well she could, but it all depended on what her attitude was like. Natalie then remembered that Patrice wanted to handle Maria and she had to respect.

"Hello, this is Natalie."

"I fucked up Nat." Maria said with a dehydrated tone to her voice. She sounded terrible. Almost as if she's been locked in a dark room for weeks. Her once sweet and innocent voice sound a little hoarse.

"Maria is that you?" Knowing that it was, but she tried to remain clueless while she seemed to get ready to confess.

"Yea Nat, it's me. I don't know what happened. Nat, I did something and I think I went overboard with it. All I was trying to do was scare him and somehow it went all wrong!"

Maria started crying and coughing at the same time and Natalie knew she was in a lot of pain.

"Maria, tell me what happened."

"Nat, you know that I'm in love with Dr. T and I can't get over the fact that he doesn't love me back. There's another woman in the picture now and that added fuel to my fire. I asked Dr. T if he would marry me and he told me no! I love this man and I don't understand what I did wrong!"

"Maria, girl you need help. You don't love Dr. T. You love that Daddy Dick he was putting on yo' ass and you need to leave him alone girl, because the truth is, he don't want you girl, never will, so you need to leave him alone. All you really love is the chase. Let's face it Maria, you always get everything you want except this. It's almost like a game to you and you need to grow up!"

Natalie couldn't help but tell it like it is. She knew Maria wasn't accustomed to being talked to like that. Maria is one of those people who thought she was better than everybody just because she had money and a body to die for.

She had all the curves a man could want. Her skin was perfect and Natalie was sure she knew what to do to make a man buckle at the knees. But she finally came across a man that buckled her ass instead and now she had a friend in Natalie, whom she thought was beneath her, telling her things she didn't want to hear.

"Whatever girl." Maria said.

"Ok, don't take my advice, but remember that you are the one calling me saying you fucked up!" \

"Whatever Nat, Dr. T loves me, but he haven't realized it yet. All I have to do is get this other woman out of the picture. Then Dr. T will see that he really does love me and he can't see himself without me!"

"It sounds like you have it all figured out Maria, but what did you do that was so bad that got you sounding like you swallowed some dirt or some shit girl?"

Natalie sat back on her couch with her legs crossed. She tried to keep herself from going off on Maria. She may be able to leave the ass beating up to Patrice, but Natalie could get some satisfaction out busting Maria's bubble about her plans.

"It all started a couple of weeks ago. Girl, I got all dressed up and shit for my papi. I wore his favorite black and red dress that shows all of my curves. I dabbed on some of my best perfume. Girl, I left out the house looking fierce and on a mission to get my man. Anyways, I was texting him and he wasn't texting me back, so I parked outside his house and I saw this little bitch walk in. Nat, I have to admit that the bitch was looking good, but she don't have shit on me ya' know? A little while later, I guess they got into an argument or something so she took off."

Natalie listed to Maria go on and on and she still haven't told her what she did, even though she already knew. She walked to the kitchen to make her something a little stronger because she was really trying to keep it all in, but Natalie was boiling inside. If she kept calling my sister a bitch, she was bound to lose it.

"Nat, I figured if I went up to his door, my papi wouldn't have opened it, so I followed this little chica to her house and told Dr. T that I was right outside her window looking dead at her. I asked him to marry me and I warned him that if he gave me the wrong answer, I would do something bad to his little girlfriend. I really wasn't going to do anything to her; I just knew that if I said that, Dr. T would drive over and try save the little bitch. So his answer was no and...."

"And what?"

"He did exactly what I expected him to, but my plan was to meet him and side swipe him a little. Ya' know? Kind of run into him a little bit, but not hurt him. The next thing I see Nat, is my Dr. T airbag explode."

"I hit him head on. It turns out I planned on hitting him from the side, but I was texting him at the time and he looked down to do something with his phone and swerved to where I ran into him head on!"

"Dayuum Maria, what about you? Did you get hurt at all?"

"Yea I got a little banged up, but it's time for me to take the little bitch out the picture...."

"Wait, Maria what are you talking about, take her out the picture?"

"Nat, I seen this little chica up at the hospital with Dr. T every single day and the short while I was there, it made me sick. Dr. T is my man. I don't have a plan as to how I'm going to get this bitch out of the picture, but whatever it is, you gon' be down with me, right mami?"

"Girl fa' sho'. Do you even have to ask? Shit, you're my best friend right?"

"That's what I'm talking about Nat, I knew I could count on you!"

Natalie knocked back a few swigs of her drank and prepared herself for bubble busting time.

"Ohhhh shit! Maria I forgot about one little thing that may be a problem."

"What is it Nat?" Maria said while giggling.

"Well do you remember me telling you about my long lost sister calling me? Well we been talking the last couple of weeks and ya' know, catching back up and shit....." Maria cut Natalie off.

"Nat, are you over there drinking? What does that have to do with anything?"

"Yes, I have been drinking, but that's not the point. There is a little problem with me helping you because...uuummm... my sister...Patrice...."

"Yes, Patrice....."

"Well, I recently found out that, my sister is in love with Dr. T and if I ever hear you call her a bitch again, I will put my foot so far up your ass that it will take something that hadn't even been invented yet to get it out!"

There was silence on the phone and Maria couldn't believe what she just heard. Natalie didn't expect her to leave Dr. T alone, just because of what she said. She's given her no hint throughout their friendship that she thought about anyone, but herself.

"Nat, what are you talking about?" Maria said with a slight giggle.

"You heard me Maria. The '*bitch*' that you are trying to get rid of is my sister and I ain't having it. She really loves him and he loves her back. It's not the kinda love that you say you have for him Maria, it's the real thing and I won't let you get in the way of that!"

"Nat, I thought you were my best friend?"

"I am Maria, but Patrice is my sister. You need to understand that if I really thought that you were in love with Dr. T, then I would stay out of it because how can I get into the middle of something between my best friend and my sister. I just think my sister genuinely loves Terry and you don't."

"Ok, who is Terry?"

"Exactly Maria, if you have to ask then it proves my point. Terry is Dr. T's real name."

"Well Nat, I'ma just put it to you like this mami, Dr. T or Terry, is my man and you know I work hard to get the things that I want. Dr. T is what I want, so if I was you, I would want to stay out of it. I'm prepared to do whatever I need to do to have that Daddy Dick in me again!"

Natalie wasn't surprised by Maria's remark, she kind of expected it. All she could tell Patrice is that they have a fight on their hands because Maria was not letting Dr. T go.

Natalie laugh to herself thinking that Daddy Dick dun' got her ass. Maria and Natalie went back and forth for about ten more minutes before she hung the phone up in Natalie's face. She stretched out on her sofa after having a few drinks and thought about some upcoming adventures that her and Patrice will have to deal with.

Chapter 28

It's now been three months that Terry has been in the hospital and Patrice was beginning to worry about him. The doctors and nurses kept advising her that he's not doing worse, but he's not doing better either.

Patrice was on her way to go see him since she hadn't visited Terry in a couple a weeks. Natalie told her to chill on visiting so often because Maria often spies on her. Patrice wasn't too concerned with Maria, but she felt that she needed to give the doctors and staff a break because she was up there every day for about two months straight.

Natalie and Patrice sold their mom's house and she moved to a different location. Patrice thought that she would always stay her mom's house, but it was just too hard for her to stay there and not have my mom with her. So, they both decided that it would be best that she moved and Maria knowing where she stayed played a factor in it too.

She walked into the hospital and practically the whole staff spoke and asked where she's been. Patrice's only response to that question was that she's been taking care of some business. One nurse in particular pulled her to the side and basically grilled her for not coming to check up on Terry in so long.

She was a sweet old lady, with shiny gray hair and had one of those grandmamma voices. Patrice

adored the little old lady, she was a couple inches shy of standing five feet tall, but she talked as if she stood seven feet tall. She had pain written all over her hands and she had a struggled walk. She had a dark complexion with wrinkles filling her face and she wore her glasses on the tip of her nose, but yet she always smiled, simply because she was alive as she would say; except for right now.

"Baby, where you been?" She asked, half way bending in pain.

"Hey Ms. Mildred, I just thought I would give you guys a break and also get some things in line for myself." Patrice said with a smile on her face, but she realized that she was the only one smiling. Ms. Mildred seemed angry and Patrice knew she would find out why.

"Don't hey Ms. Mildred me chile, why are you here?"

"Ms. Mildred, I'm here to check up on Terry."

"Honey, another lady been coming up here checking up on that man. I thought you couldn't handle it since you haven't been up here in a while. I really don't like that baby too much either chile. Let me tell ya', she is rude and just evil, but I'm just gon' let the lawd take care of it. That's right, I'm putting it in God's hands chile."

Just like that, the smile was wiped off her face. There was another woman that's been there watching over Terry. She shifted her purse into her other hand and began to walk off, but Ms. Mildred followed her.

"Ms. Mildred, who is this other lady and how well do you guys know her?" Patrice asked while walking to Terry's room.

"Baby, all I know is that when you stopped coming, this other chile started coming. We wondered what happened to you, hell; I even called you a couple times myself." Ms. Mildred is a sweet old lady, but she can curse something vicious if she gets mad enough.

"I'm sorry Ms. Mildred, but I moved and got my number changed. I felt I needed to do it. Why does everyone dislike this new lady?"

"Shit, for one, she ain't you. I just can't stand that rude mutha fucka baby. Excuse Ms. Mildred's language, but I just don't like the heffa!"

Patrice wanted to laugh so bad, but she held it in because she was a little curious of who this lady was.

"Ms. Mildred, how is Terry doing? Please tell me that he is doing better?"

"Awww that baby is improving a lot chile, but don't leave it to Ms. Mildred to explain everything that's going on with that man. Tell me something honey, what's the deal with you and that man? Is that yo' man baby?"

"That's a long story Ms. Mildred, too long to......" Ms. Mildred cut her off just like that.

"That's the problem with these young people. Chile, in my day, when an elder ask you a question, you best give an answer. Now answer me dammit. What's the deal with you and that man in there? Before you answer, let me tell you that he's been talking and all he seems to......."

"Wait! Wait, Ms. Mildred, you said he's been talking. Terry's talking now? That means he's doing better right?"

Patrice damn near tripped over herself to ask Ms. Mildred about Terry. She couldn't believe he was talking now. All she wanted to do was put her arms around him and tell him she loved him and to hear him say it back. Who was she kidding, he's her Terry and he will always be her Terry. Instantly the smile returned to her face and there was nothing that could take it away, not even Ms. Mildred's strong vocabulary.

"Yes he's talking now, and you betta stop interrupting me chile while I'm talking. I was saying that all he seemed to talk about was you. If I was you, I wouldn't get too excited cuz he stopped talking bout you since you haven't been here in a month. Like I was saying, what's going on with y'all baby?" Patrice stood there like she did when her mom would grill her about something.

"Well Ms. Mildred, we were in love with each other. I told him and he told me that he loved me. It was the beginning of something big and special. I loved

Terry like I never loved anyone. He loved me like I was the only person that mattered to him and no one has ever loved me that way except my mom and dad, both are in heaven right now."

"I'm sorry to hear about your mom and dad, but baby give me the good stuff. Now, don't get me wrong, it's good to hear how in love y'all were, but I wanna hear about what's going on now."

Patrice paused for awhile because Ms. Mildred was having her live that night over again and she felt that she moved on from that horrible night.

"I went over to Terry's house one night….the same night that we shared with each other that we loved each other and it started out to be a very special night. I told him some things about me that he needed to know, really that I needed him to know about me. We started getting pretty intimate and I was going to make love to him and Ms. Mildred, it would have been my first time."

"Ok chile, so what happened?"

"Well right before it was about to happen, Terry stopped and said that he needed to share something with me. He told me that he basically had an alter ego and this meant that he slept with a bunch of women including my sister. Terry told me that he became this way because of what one woman did to him. All he wanted to do was make sure every woman was treated as such and felt as if they were queens. Terry said that he had a gift to give any and every woman what they desired. He claimed that all of this happened before he met me. Terry went on to explain that he slept with my sister before he met me and she was one of the one's that he helped. I can say that she is totally different from how I remembered her before. How can I be with a man that's done what he's done Ms. Mildred?"

"Baby, I've only known you a short while, but when I say this, just know that it's out of respect. You are dumb as hell, yall young ladies are just dumb baby. Now Ms. Mildred don't mean you're really dumb, I just mean yall don't know no betta. Anyone can see that Terry was telling you the truth. If he wasn't, that man would have slept with you and took your virginity, then told you what he had to tell you. Something tells me that he is in here because of you. Not that it's your fault, but I have a feeling you are a part of it."

Ms. Mildred and Patrice both stood outside Terry's room talking and she made her look at the situation in a way that she hadn't thought about. Terry knew she was a virgin and that she was saving herself for marriage, but she was ready to make love to him that night and he knew it.

Still he did not go through with it until he told Patrice something that he obviously felt she should know before they took that step. Ms. Mildred made Patrice realize that Terry wanted to make sure that she would still be with him, even after he told her about this Dr. T thing. She would have felt horrible if she made love to Terry and then found out later about this Dr. T situation.

They stood and talked for awhile longer and Ms. Mildred took both of Patrice's hands and held them tight while looking her dead in her eyes with concern.

"Baby, that man loves you. He wakes up every morning calling out for someone named babygirl and my gut is telling me that you are babygirl. Am I right?"

"Yes, he calls me babygirl." Patrice began crying right away.

"Oh baby, wipe them tears away. It's too late to think about what you could have done different. Everything we go through and will go through is already planned out for us chile, so don't worry about what could have been and just start thinking about what you gon' do about it!"

Finally, Ms. Mildred cracked a smile at Patrice after she gave her a hug. Patrice stood there and watched her as she walked away and she laughed to herself.

Patrice walked into Terry's room and she saw him talking to James.

James turned to Patrice and turned back without even speaking to her as if she's done something wrong. She walked over to Terry and before she got to him, James got up and stopped her.

"James what is wrong with you?" Patrice asked nervously.

"Hey Patrice, something is wrong with Terry and I thought I should warn you before you talk to him."

Shit, what is it now Patrice thought. James had a sad and scared look on his face which scared her even more because the few times that she's seen James, he seemed quite confident.

"James, what's wrong with him now?"

"I don't really know how to say this, but something has gone wrong. I was here with Terry about two weeks ago and he seemed to be doing great. He was talking, mostly about you. He wanted to know where you were and why wasn't you around, but a couple of days later I noticed that he started talking like Dr. T use to talk."

"What are you talking about James?"

"Well Terry and Dr. T have a different kind of swagger to them. I could always tell whether I was talking to Terry or Dr. T."

"James, what are you trying to say?" James put his head down and seemed like he was about to start crying.

"I don't think he remembers you Patrice. I asked the doctors what happened. One day he can't stop talking about you and suddenly he doesn't remember anything about you."

"James, I don't believe it. Are you serious? I'll just go find out for myself because he has to remember me!"

Patrice started to head over Terry's way until James grabbed her and pulled her back once again. She didn't understand why this was happening this way. After talking to Ms. Mildred, she finally realized that they belonged together.

She understood that Terry was only looking out for her and was trying to be completely honest with her.

Patrice realized she couldn't live without her Terry and now he doesn't remember who she is.

She wasn't sure how to love someone who loves her, only he doesn't remember that he loves her. What other obstacles was she suppose to get over and how many things would God continue to put her through?

She's been through a lot and was still going through it. She lost her mom, found love in the process and reconciled with her lost sister, then found out that the man she loved slept with her sister and he has a crazy stalker who put him up in the hospital.

"Let me go James, I have to find this out for myself!" Patrice screamed.

James watched her as she walked over to Terry and he looked as if he just saw someone commit suicide.

"Terry….."

"Hi….."

"How are you doing?"

"I'm doing good ok, I guess. The doctors told me I was in a coma for about two months. So I guess I'm good and rested up."

"How are you feeling?"

"I feel good. I'm just ready to get out of here."

"Well I'm glad you're feeling good Terry."

"Please don't be upset with me, but the doctors told me I may have some memory loss and I hate to ask this question, but do I know you?"

Patrice's heart sank as she watched this man, the man that she loved and the man that loved her, look her dead in the face and ask who she was. Her heart exploded into pieces while she sat on the bed with him wondering if she really wanted to convince Terry of remembering her.

Terry apologized over and over again for not remembering her, but still her heartbeat didn't beat the same. Her eyes didn't see the world the same. Her ears couldn't detect love in her man's voice anymore.

Terry had become all that she had ever wanted and needed. She wasn't sure how she was supposed to go on knowing he didn't remember her.

He kept apologizing and Patrice could tell that he genuinely felt bad because he knew she was hurting. He knew something was wrong with her, he knew she had just lost something. Terry listened to Patrice with love and care, which she appreciated, but he spoke to her like a stranger getting to know someone.

Patrice kept thinking about what Ms. Mildred said and she refused to give up on Terry. She still needed to find out who the other lady was that's been visiting Terry. Patrice gave him a hug and he whispered in her ear that everything will work itself out the way it supposed to be and he wiped away her tears. That was the Terry she knew, but it made her happy and pissed off at the same time.

James gave Patrice a hug and told her that it will get better. She walked out of Terry's room, flipped on her shades and she knew that a different Patrice was walking out of the hospital. She was determined to get her man back. She was angry and Maria will be sorry that she fucked with Patrice and her man.

Chapter 29
Dr. T

It's been a few a couple of weeks since I've been home from the hospital and I just thank God that I'm back. Things were starting to get back to normal and I have my first appointment tonight.

So I begin setting the mood, just like I use to do, but before anything, I pour me some Brandy. Instantly, the Brandy slid down my throat smooth and it relaxed my mind so I didn't have a worry in the world. I jumped in the shower and I couldn't believe how peaceful my Brandy had me right now.

I stood butt ass naked in the shower, letting the water explode in my face and it felt dayum good too. I was having thoughts of a beautiful woman joining me in the shower.

She's gorgeous with long, black, silky hair and luscious caramel skin. Her eyes were a deep shade of brown. Whoever this woman was, she knew what she doing. She kissed me on my neck and tasted the water as it dripped down to my chest and a new goose bump was made every time her lips touched my body.

My abs received kisses from her lips that mixed in by her tongue and I started to go crazy. Then slowly, she made her way down to my dick which she grabbed with both of her hands, licking and kissing around my balls and up my shaft. She opened wide to stuff her mouth on my dick and just like that, I was awakened from my daydream.

My dick remained hard as I jumped out of the shower and I walked around my house naked until my dick decided to go down. I took a couple shots of my Brandy and played some of my R. Kelly that helped me relax even more. Finally, my dick went down and I started to put on some clothes. Nothing special, just some sweatpants and a T-shirt, along with my '*fuckem*' cologne. Just as I walked back into the living room, my door bell rang.

"Come on in baby."

"Hey Dr. T, it's been a long time hasn't it?"

All I could see was a fat ass and perfect breasts. This beautiful lady walked past me, having me inhale the essence of her scent that made me instantly want to taste the sweet nectar of her juices. I wanted my tongue to play in her garden and I wanted my hands to rub her ass like it was a crystal ball.

"Baby just go and sit on the couch and I'll be right there."

"Anything for you Papi!"

Maria was back in my life and I'm glad she was. She's the only one who came to see me besides James, but in the back of my head, I still wondered about the lady that came in to visit me. Patrice. She was beautiful and I only wished I could remember who she was.

"Maria, do you want something to drink?"

"I'll take what you're having Papi."

Maria and I talked for a little bit, but with the amount of liquor we both had, we started doing what we do best, fuck. I watched as Maria stood up, she took off her top and her breasts begged for me to touch and kiss them, but I didn't give in to her begs.

With my dick hard as stone and pointing straight out, Maria knew she was going to have some Daddy Dick in her tonight. I slowly walked up on her and had my dick stroke her ass.

"Papi, stop teasing me with that Daddy Dick."

Do you want Daddy Dick?"

"Yes, papi you know I want it."

Maria eyes squinted as she imagined Daddy Dick plunging in and out of her pussy. Her mouth never closed as if she was envisioning me taste testing her. Maria bent over my sofa and her tasty nice center opening screamed for me to enter. She then stood, only in her red stilettos and business skirt. I finished undressing Maria and turned her around to warm up her insides and to get her strawberry juices flowing. And strawberry was definitely my favorite.

My tongue entered the residence of Maria's pussy and I took my own tour. I inspected every bit of her garden and she rewarded me by quenching my thirst with her splash waterfall of juices. I was tasting and swallowing all I could and more.

"Ohhh….oh my God Papi…shit I'm about to come, fuck!"

I continued feasting on Maria and dayum, I thought the Brandy was intoxicating, I was so ready to start fucking Maria, but I couldn't tear my tongue away from her pussy. Maria came twice with me just licking and sucking away.

"Bend over for me baby."

Maria followed directions beautifully and I watched as she bent over and her breasts hung over the sofa. Her mouth was already opened wide and it got wider as she felt Daddy Dick part through her pussy lips.

"Papi….Papi….Paaaaappppi…..Daddy Dick feels so dayuum good!"

Maria wanted it fast, deep and hard. I delivered Daddy Dick just the way she wanted and sometimes I would slow up my stroke just so she could feel every inch of Daddy Dick going inside of her and then to feel the sensation of me going fast, deep and hard again drove her crazy.

Maria came again after I flipped her over onto her back and put her legs on my shoulder, which allowed me to go deeper. Maria screamed and yelled loud in my ear, but she was only responding to something I was doing to and for her. I exploded inside Maria and felt the magnum condom catch my seeds like a baseball glove.

Maria was lying on the couch exhausted, but very satisfied and her hair was not fixed in the sexy ponytail that she had when she rung the door bell. Instead it hung, long and sweaty over her exhausted face.

"Papi, that was incredible. I can do this with you forever Papi."

"What are you trying to say Maria?"

"Relax papi, I'm just saying I enjoy what we do. Can I ask you a question?"

Maria was still the same, she always wanted a deep conversation afterwards and I just wanted her to go home or be quiet afterwards. I don't usually be this way with my clients, but Maria is different. She sees an opportunity and she runs with it, she don't seem to know when enough is enough and I just learned to be stern with her, basically control her.

"Maria, if you have any questions about what my plans are for settling down, then you can skip it."

"Fine, but how did you know what I was going to ask you?"

"Look, I realize I had some loss of memory, but I still remember you and how you are."

I couldn't believe that Maria tried to take advantage of my situation like that, but then again, I wasn't too surprised. We went back and forth until she knew I wasn't biting.

Maria's necklace was tangled up in her hair and she had only one stiletto heel on, hopping around looking for the other one. She had an incredible body and just to be able to look at her was great. She had the perfect Kim Kardashian ass and Tyra Banks breasts, just a beautiful Latino. Maria bit down on hair pins as she fixed her ponytail back up and soon she will be on and out.

"Thank you papi, I had a great time."

"No problem, it's always a pleasure pleasing you, but it's about time I take my medicine and get some rest."

"Ok Dr. T, I can take a hint."

"I'm glad you can!" I said jokingly, but halfway serious.

"Ha ha papi, very funny."

"Ok Maria, just call me when you want to get together again."

"Will do Dr. T and I'm so glad that you are feeling better. I will talk to you soon."

"Goodbye Maria." I kissed Maria on the cheek and watched her other cheeks sashay down my drive way.

Chapter 30
Terry

It's been a couple of weeks since I started back messing with Maria again and I slept with her a few times since then and also some past clients. It was starting to get old to me and I started thinking about family life again.

I tend to always wonder when I'm going to settle down for real and have some kids of my own. Like I always tell Maria, stop questioning what can't be explained.

I called up JB because he seems to be the only that knows how to get me out of these kind of moods.

"Hello?"

"JB, what's up man, it's been awhile since I heard from you man. What's going on?"

"What's up?" JB replied, real short and soft tone.

"What's wrong, you ok man?"

"Yeah, I'm good. How are you feeling?"

"I'm doing well, I'm just in one of those moods where I'm thinking about family and kids again."

"Well, you should be thinking about it." Something wasn't right with JB; usually he would have cracked some kind of joke or something. Instead, he was being very direct and short with me.

"Seriously JB, what's wrong? You know I know when something wrong with you so spill it!"

"Ok, Terry it's like this. I think you fucking up big time messing around with Maria. I keep telling you that she is the reason that you ended up in the hospital that night. I know you don't remember some things, but you keep running around here talking about how you want to settle down and have a family of your own. I was proud of you Terry because you were finally heading in that way with Patrice. Again, I know you don't remember, but Patrice was there with you pretty much the whole time when you were in a coma. Maria only started coming around when you started showing some improvement and if you ask me, I believe that she is the reason that you're having some memory loss."

"Why do you think that JB, how can she cause me to have some memory loss?"

"I don't know, but even you said yourself that she would do anything to get what she wants and it's just such a coincidence that you don't remember certain things, mainly Patrice. You were in love with this woman and she was in love with you."

"JB, if she was so in love with me, then why wasn't she there when I was getting better. I only remember seeing you and Maria."

"Dammit Terry, why in the hell would I lie to you about some shit like this!"

JB hardly ever cursed at me, which kind of gave me reason to believe that there was some truth to what he was saying, but he has no truth and all I can go on right now is what I remember.

"Watch your tone with me JB, I never said that you were lying. I just can't see myself going to this Patrice woman based on what you guys are telling me. I am Dr. T, and I will continue to be Dr. T until that special woman comes along and steals my heart. JB, you know what my goal is, it's to make every woman feel like the queens and princesses that they are."

"Brutha, I get that, I honestly do, but you are robbing yourself of your own happiness."

"I don't believe I am JB, because seeing these women happy makes me happy."

"Fine Terry, but what if I can prove it to you?"

"Prove what to me?"

"What if I can prove that Maria set all this up and that you and Patrice were falling in love?"

"JB, do what you have to do, but as of right now I am Dr. T and I just want my best friend back, can I have that?"

"Aight man, whateva. Terry I have to go take care some things, I'll talk to you later, aight?"

"Ok JB, later."

I could tell that JB was a little upset, but how am I suppose to stop being me based on something I don't even remember happening. I do remember Patrice visiting me in the hospital and I remember feeling horrible that I didn't remember her because she is gorgeous. She had long, black, wavy hair and her smile made the inside of me smile for just that moment.
I was interrupted in mid thought by a number I didn't recognize. Normally I wouldn't answer numbers I didn't know, but since there's a lot I didn't remember, I decided to answer.

"Hello?"

"Hi Terry." A sweet voice said.

"Hi."

"How are you?" She responded as if I was supposed to recognize her.

"I'm doing good. I'm wondering who I'm speaking to, but other than that, I'm doing good."

"It's Patrice crazy." She laughed.

"Oh ok, hey Patrice, how are you doing? Thanks for coming to visit me. I only remember seeing you that one time, but I've been told that you were there a lot."

"I'm doing ok. Yea, I was there so much I actually was getting on the staff's nerves. I'm sorry I haven't called you in a while, but you have to understand how hard this is for me. I have to talk to you and you don't even know who I am. I basically have to get to know you all over again."

"I understand and it's hard on my end too with people telling me that I was doing this and I was doing that with this person when I don't even remember."

Patrice had the sweetest voice that God has ever made. When she spoke, she sung to my heart and I was a little embarrassed by it.

"Well Terry, I know it's a little late, but I actually called to see if you wanted to go somewhere with me tonight. It's just a night out together. I'm not going to try to get you to remember anything or talk about anything you don't want to talk about."

"How can I turn down an invitation with a beautiful woman? Where do you want to go?"

"Well, I was thinking one of my favorite spots. Have you ever heard of Shania's?"

"Yes Patrice, I have and actually, that's one of my favorite spots to just sit back and relax."

"Ok I'll get dressed and meet you over."

"See you when I get there."

"Ok, good bye Terry."

Just like that, she was off the phone and I was headed to the shower once again. I was like a teenager getting ready for a date. I was so excited and nervous at the same time. I lay out my nice black pin stripe suit with a matching Kangol hat to match.

After my quick shower, I quickly shaved and trimmed up my goatee until it was sharp. Just like that I was dressed and grabbing the keys to my Lincoln Mark truck and jamming some R. Kelly while on my way to Shania's. We practically arrived at the same time and I saw this beautiful lady walk up to me and start speaking.

"Hey Terry, glad you can make it."

Shit! Patrice was beautiful, just stunning. She wore a shiny red dress that clung perfectly to her body and her hair was long and wavy slightly hanging over her right shoulder. I couldn't help but watch her glossy lips part ways as she opened her mouth to speak to me.

I wanted my lips to be connected to hers.

"I'm glad to be here Patrice."

The night pretty much started off kind of quiet. We listened to some nice soft music and the only communication between us was Patrice's occasional head turn toward with a smile. She rocked slowly, back and forth to the music and I watched her movement and paid close attention to it. I normally could tell how a woman liked to be touched and held just by the way she moved to music.

"Patrice?"

"Yes Terry?"

"Would you like to dance with me?" I asked nervously.

"I would love to Terry."

I got up from my seat and took Patrice's hand while leading her to the dance floor. We were the only two people out there dancing and I was sure neither one of us minded. We danced to one of my favorite songs. *Always and Forever* by Heat Wave, I just loved that song.

"You don't mind if I sing along to this do you Patrice?"

"No, not at all." she laughed.

"Good, I promise I won't embarrass you."

'Always and Forever, each moment with you , it's just like a dream to me, that somehow came true and I know tomorrow, will still be the same, cuz we got a life of love, that won't ever change and every day, love me your own special way, melt all my heart away with a smile, take time to tell me, you really care, and we'll share tomorrow, together, I'll always love you, forever.'

"Ok, I'll stop now. I just really love old songs Patrice."

"So do I Terry and I loved your singing."

I held Patrice close to me and she laid her head on my chest while I rubbed her back slowly.

"Can I tell you something silly Patrice?" I whispered.

"Yea Terry."

"Well, it's not really silly, but I just want to share it with you. I was talking to my friend James today and… and…"

"And what Terry?" I got quiet and couldn't believe I started this conversation.

"Well he got a little upset with me because of some things that I'm doing with my life."

"Like what Terry?"

I figured I might as well tell Patrice about this Dr. T thing, but then again, we were having such a good time and I didn't want to ruin it.

"Never mind Patrice, I don't want to ruin the night that we are having."

"Are you sure Terry?"

"Yes I'm sure."

"Well, I'll just say this Terry. I know a lot about you already. I know about your past and who you were and what you did and when you told me about the Dr. T thing, I ran out on you. I just didn't know how to deal with knowing that you slept with my sister, Natalie, but I'm over that now because I know your reasoning for doing that and also I realize that all that happened before you met me. So I'm ready to move past that whole Dr. T thing."

Ok, what the hell just happened and how she knew about Dr. T, I thought. If she knew about Dr. T then there has to be some kind of truth to what JB was saying.

"Wait, wait. So you know about Dr. T and Maria and the clients that I had?"

"Yes Terry I know about all of them and you told me that it was before we met, so I chose to deal with it. Not at first, but I realize that if I really loved you, I have to trust in what you tell me."

Shit, my head was spinning and I was confused.

"Baby, we need to go talk. I need to tell you something and it's very important that you hear me out."

"Ok Terry, what is it?"

I rushed Patrice back over to the table and quickly drank my Brandy and Coke. I wasn't sure how Patrice was going to take this, but I thought it was important that she knew Dr. T had come back. It was obvious that she thought he had gone.

"Well Patrice, I don't really know how to tell you this, but you know that I've had some memory loss and with that, there are some things I remember and some things that I just don't. I don't remember you coming to visit me at all in the hospital and I'm not angry with you about that, I'm just saying that I didn't know you to expect you to visit me, if that makes sense."

"Yes, it makes sense Terry, but you…"

"Wait Patrice, please let me finish. You seem to be aware of whom Maria is and she is the person that I remember being at the hospital with me a lot. So she helped me remember who I was and what was going on before the accident. I'm glad you know about the Dr. T situation so I don't have to explain that, but as far as me no longer being Dr. T. I haven't stopped, I'm sorry, but I have to be honest with you and……"

Patrice began crying as she interrupted me.

"Terry, what are you trying to say? Please don't tell me that you and…..Maria and you been…..you are back being Dr. T!"

Patrice ran out of Shania's crying and I had to follow her and make sure she was ok. I couldn't stand that fact that this woman was hurting. All I ever want to do was keep women from hurting and this is the one time that being Dr. T was hurting a woman.

"Patrice wait!"

"What is it Terry? What do you have to say? Excuse me, not Terry; what do you have to say Dr. T?"

"Patrice, I had to be honest with you, you can't blame me for something if I don't remember it happening."

"Well, Dr. T baby, don't call me until you figure this shit out and realize what you really want, but I want you to understand something, I am not, and I repeat, I am not going to wait for you to get it. Goodbye!"

Chapter 31

Each day without talking to or hearing from Terry was getting harder and harder. In a screwed up way, she kind of regretted the way she went off on him a couple of weeks ago. Like he said, it wasn't his fault that a crazy bitch put him up in a hospital and now he has short term memory loss.

Patrice missed her Terry so much and she hoped that he was doing well and she wanted him to realize that he didn't have to be Dr. T anymore.

She's been lying in her bed crying everyday for the last two weeks and she didn't see anything getting better until Terry got his memory back. Natalie had called her about five times this morning alone and she kept calling. Patrice wanted to be left alone, especially with her crying her eyes out right now. After about five more calls, she finally answered the phone.

"Hello?"

"Trice' get up right now, get dressed. Now!" Natalie screamed into Patrice's ear.

"Nat, what is this about?"

"Girl, the hospital and police have been trying to get in touch with you, but yo' ass dun went and got your number changed and moved!"

"What for? What happened now?"

Patrice couldn't take any more bad news. She received bad news after bad news and couldn't deal with it anymore.

"Trice' get yo ass up girl. Do you remember when you told the police to check Terry's phone records?"

"Yea, so what?"

"Shit girl. They checked all the texts that Maria sent Terry and now they have a warrant out for her arrest. They now believe that Maria caused that fucked up accident. Not only that girl, but the doctors called me, when they couldn't get a hold of you. They have some suspicion that Terry was drugged while he was in a coma!"

"Wait Nat' are you serious? So now what?"

"Like I said, get yo' ass up cuz I'm on my way!" Just like that, Patrice got out of bed and took a quick shower.

She sipped on the cup of coffee that she made after she got dressed, looked down at her phone and saw that Terry was calling. Patrice wondered if anyone told him about this news of Maria. She even thought about not answering it, but couldn't help it.

"Hello?"

"Hey Patrice, it's me, Terry."

"Hey Terry, how are you doing?"

"I'm doing ok, I just thought I would check up on you since I haven't heard from you in a while."

"Terry, do you still talk to Maria?"

"Yes, I talk to her. Why do you ask?"

"Well, have you gotten a call from the police or the hospital?"

"No Patrice, I haven't. Can you please tell me what this is all about?"

She wasn't sure what this was all about and Patrice really didn't want to be the one to tell him. She knew that he will think that she was making it all up and plus she didn't really have enough information herself.

"It's nothing Terry, I was just checking to see if you heard anything about the accident investigation or if you heard any news from the hospital."

"I haven't heard anything, but I need to talk to you about something pretty serious." Suddenly, Patrice's ears perked up and she turned around in chair as if that would make her listen harder.

"What is it Terry?"

"I don't know why I'm calling you and bothering you with this, but when I picked my phone up, I dialed your number."

"You are not bothering me Terry, what's going on?"

Natalie was outside knocking on the door, but Patrice ignored the knocks so she could hear what Terry had to say.

"Well, I think I'm starting to remember certain things. It's things that I may have dreamed about, but it don't make any sense to me and I was hoping that maybe you can try to explain it to me."

Patrice tried her best to keep her excitement of Terry's memory coming back, to herself. She was listening hard and Natalie was beating on the door, screaming for Patrice to let her in.

She walked over to the door and let Natalie in, but she held her finger up to her mouth signaling for Natalie to be quiet.

"Talk to me Terry, maybe I can help?"

Patrice emphasized Terry's name so that Natalie knew to keep quiet.

"Well, I keep having a reoccurring dream and it's about me in heaven talking to my mom and dad. I remember something about me mentioning to her I was in love with someone, but I never mentioned a name to her and I'm trying to figure out who that person is. Not only that Patrice, I had also seen this old lady who looked very familiar to me. Patrice, it's been killing me for the last week to figure out what all of this means. I remember you saying that you knew a lot about me and that we were falling in love with each other, but what I guess I need from you is to tell me everything that happened between us and maybe things will start to make sense."

"Terry, why would you trust someone that you don't know to tell you something?"

"Patrice, if there was some love there with you, I should be able to trust in what you tell me and trust that you won't tell me anything that didn't exist."

"I guess what I'm really wanting to know is if you are ready to hear the truth Terry?"

"Patrice, I'm begging you to tell me something, please."

Tears were starting to pour prematurely because Patrice knew it would be hard for her to relive everything that she and Terry had been through. It would also hurt because she knew it wouldn't fix things completely. She wanted and needed Terry to remember things on his own.

"Patrice, are you there?"

"Yes Terry, I'm here."

"Never mind Patrice, I have an important call that I need to take. Can we talk about this later; if there is a later."

"Terry wait! I'll tell you, but you have to know that it's hard for me." Patrice screamed.

"Patrice, I have to go. This is the hospital that is waiting and it may be something important. We'll talk about it later."

"Ok, bye Terry." Patrice whimpered like a sad little girl as the tears trickled with disappointment down her face.

"Bye Patrice."

Terry hung the phone up, but she held it to her ear like she was expecting him to come back, but he never did. Natalie walked over to her and put her arm around Patrice, which made her cry more.

"Natalie, I'm just tired of crying over this man!" "Trice', no you're not. You are just tired of crying of this situation."

Patrice cried to Natalie, asking her why she had to be so damn stubborn. Terry basically asked for her help and she acted like an ass. Patrice could have really helped him out and herself if she would have told him everything. Natalie tried her best to calm Patrice down and she did a little bit.

"Yea Trice', you were a little stubborn, but understand that you will have other chances and yo' ass

better take advantage of it next time. I don't mean to sound like I'm rushing you, but we really need to get moving to the hospital to see what these doctors are talking about."

Natalie helped Patrice wash her face and get everything back together. She put her sunglasses on a said 'let's go find out what this bitch did to yo' man girl!'

Chapter 32
Terry

I felt horrible about how I got off the phone with Patrice, but it was her fault. I asked her more than once to give me some information that could help me and she stalled while an important call came in that I had to take.

"Hello?"

"May I speak to Mr. Davis?"

"Speaking."

"Hi Mr. Davis, this is Dr. Wolciek. I was calling to give you some information. It has something to do with your short term memory loss."

"Ok, good. Dr. Wolciek, will my short term memory loss be permanent?"

"Hold on my friend, we're getting ahead of ourselves.

Dr. Wolciek was a cool doctor, but he had a very thick accent and he talked very slow. I think it was so he could understand himself.

"Mr. Davis, something told me to go back and review your charts because I didn't understand how everything was going as scheduled, then all of a sudden, you have memory loss. Before I go any further Mr. Davis, I think I should tell you face to face what's really going on. Do you think you can come up to the hospital so I can show you exactly what I found?"

"No problem Dr. Wolciek, I will be up there within the hour."

"Ok, I will see you then my friend."

I hung up with Dr. Wolciek and it was times like this where I really needed a drink, but I decided against it. I was getting dressed to go to the hospital and I realized I definitely didn't want to go alone so I called up my best friend to see if he wanted to ride with me.

"Yo' this is JB."

"What's up JB, this is Terry?"

"Nigga, don't you realize that people got caller ID, you don't have to tell me who it is cuz I already know!" JB said laughing.

"I see somebody is in a better mood today."

"Man Terry, I'm sorry about all that, but it's just frustrating to hear you talk about family and shit, when I know that you was getting ready to have all of that. Yo' fucked up memory is in the way of you believing it."

"That's why I called JB. My doctor called and told me that he wants me to come down to the hospital because he thinks something went wrong. I wanted to know if you can come with me because I can't do this by myself."

"Fa sho man, just come scoop me up."

Finally JB and I walked into the hospital and I almost threw up from the hospital smell. It wasn't a bad smell, it's just that I got sick of that smell from being here so long.

"Man, ain't that Patrice and Natalie up there?" JB elbowed me and pointed up ahead. He was right, it was Patrice and Natalie. Dayum Patrice is sexy. She stood there in jeans and a Dallas Cowboys sweatshirt on. Her hair was pulled back in a ponytail and she was scoping out the place, looking from side to side until her eyes found mine.

For some reason, I still remember a little bit about Natalie and I can't believe how good she looked.

"Patrice, what are you guys doing here? Don't get me wrong, I'm happy to see you. Natalie, I haven't seen you in a long time and you look good girl!"

Natalie had lost some weight and she was a nice, thick piece of beauty.

"Terry, the doctor called for me to come up here because he said that he has some suspicion that you were drugged."

"Ok, all of that is fine, but why did he call you?"

"I keep trying to tell you Terry that I was here every day when you were admitted in here. I was the one that they called and I was the one that watched over you every single day. I keep telling you that, maybe you will believe me now!"

"Patrice, calm down, I was just asking a question because I didn't know."

That's another issue I was having with this short term memory loss. When I ask a question that may seem like I'm being smart or acting like an ass, I'm really just asking the question because I don't know the answer. Every time I asked Patrice a question, she snapped on me like I should know the answer already.

"Patrice, can you please understand that when I ask you a question, I really don't know the answer to it, so please stop snapping on me!"

Patrice apologized and Dr. Wolciek came out to speak to us about what was going on.

We all went to the waiting area and sat down to hear what Dr. Wolciek had to tell us. I sat in between Patrice and Natalie, while JB stood, leaning against the wall with his hand on his chin.

"Mr. Davis, when I spoke to you on the phone. I let you know that something wasn't right with this situation. I was monitoring your situation very closely.

Your girlfriend here made sure I monitored you closely." He laughed and pointed at Patrice.

"Like I was telling you on the phone, I couldn't understand what happened to you from one day to the next. So I pulled some labs of your blood work, I pulled your blood work from when you were still in your coma and I pulled some from when you were out of your coma and back communicating."

"What I found Mr. Davis is a very, very high amount of Xanax in your system. A side effect of

Xanax is, of course, short term memory loss. I checked with all the doctors and nurses that worked on you and none of them gave you Xanax. That's why I have a suspicion you were drugged."

We all sat there with our mouths open wide and the girls had tears falling from their eyes.

"Dr. Wolciek, the only people I remember visiting was my best friend and Maria. Patrice visited me once, but by time she visited me, I had already loss my short term memory. So it had to be one of your doctors right?"

Patrice cried out, "No Terry." while shaking her head.

"Mr. Davis, how well do you know this Maria lady?" Dr. Wolciek asked.

"I know her very well Dr. Wolciek, it couldn't have been her."

"Well Mr. Davis, I believe that it was her and I have proof. You see, we have cameras in all of our rooms, so if we have an incident, we can just go back and review the tapes. I'm sorry to say Mr. Davis, but she is seen on camera dropping pills into your water and making you drink it."

"Not only that Mr. Davis, but the police gave me something to give to Patrice, but I think you should read it. In the midst of all the bad news, there is some good news Mr. Davis. I looked at your file after the memory loss and your brain activity does not show any signs of it being permanent. It will just take some time and hard work for you to gain what you've forgotten. I will leave you guys alone now to deal with this and I hope this news was good news."

Dr. Wolciek walked off and we were all frozen still. No one moved. The mood around us was tense and damn near scary. JB had his head down like always, but this time was a little different because not only did he have his head down, but it seemed he struggled to even look my way. Natalie's eyes wandered off in a direction other than where I was and she just shook her head in disbelief. Her tears ran down her face, trying their best to escape the pain that caused them to form.

Patrice sat next to me and I was hurting more, simply because she was hurt. It's amazing that I have a connection with her this deep and I'm starting to remember exactly how deep it was.

People prayed all their life for the kind of chemistry that Patrice and I shared. I'm hurting because she's hurt that someone hurt me. That's real love to me, but being hurt by another woman wouldn't allow me to see that and understand that completely.

"Natalie and JB, can you guys give me and Patrice a moment?"

Both JB and Natalie walked off together and I just sat there next to Patrice for a couple of minutes, silent. I felt betrayed, once again by another woman. I was angry and for the first time in my life, I was ready to kill a bitch.

Patrice knew I was boiling hot and she tried her best to calm me down. She put her head on my shoulder and wrapped her arms around me, rubbing my arms up and down.

"Patrice, I don't understand. I do all I can to love women and I keep getting burned. I live to put smiles on women faces and yet they still tear my heart to pieces."

Patrice wiped away some tears and planted her head on my arm while I contemplated what I would do if I ever came across Maria.

"Terry, we all search for love and the reward for real love is in the risk that we take to get it. You're not looking for love with these clients of Dr. T so why do you care if you get hurt or not. I thought that you are putting their needs before you own. Now if you're actually looking for the real thing with these women, then I could understand your frustration."

Patrice and I were just alike, she knew me and from what I was starting to remember, I knew her just as well. She knew I wasn't looking for what Dr. T was getting, which was great sex with random women to make them feel good. Patrice knew I wanted the one person that I couldn't live without and give everything that I give to all these women, to one special lady.

"Terry can I answer the question that you asked me earlier?" Patrice begged with a slight demand attached to her tone.

"Patrice, I've had a lot on my mind today so I really don't know what I asked you. Refresh my memory." I said without even making eye contact with Patrice.

I stared at a blank space in the air and had a look in my eye that if it spoke, everyone would be too scared to listen, except Patrice.

"You wanted me to tell you everything that happened between us and I want to tell you right now. Terry I think I can solve a lot of questions that you may have."

"Patrice, please stop. I begged you earlier to tell me everything and all you did was make me regret coming to you for that information. Right now, I don't even care if I remember what I forgot or not!"

"You don't care Terry? Really, you don't?" Patrice asked as she stood right in front of me.

"No Patrice, I don't. I'm tired of all of this shit, I don't deserve any of it and all I want to do right now is go find this bitch Maria.

"Terry, I understand that you are mad and angry right now, but you need to watch what you are saying to me because just like you have some shit going on in your life, so do I and I don't plan on continuing this argument. All I want to do is help and give you this information that you asked about!"

Another thing Patrice knew about me is that, whether I'm Dr. T or Terry, I can't deal with a woman crying and Patrice was pouring on the water works.

"Terry please don't be like this to me. I'm only trying to help you. Why can't you see that?"

Patrice was kneeling down in front of me crying her heart out to me and I couldn't take down the wall that was put up because of what these women kept doing to me.

"Patrice, I do understand that you are here to help me, but I just can't deal with this right now. I have to figure this out and I need to do it alone."

I stood up and proceeded to walk off and Patrice was having none of that. She was willing to fight for me, but all I had on my mind was finding Maria. It happened right there in the hospital, a big confrontation, not between me and Maria, but between Patrice and I.

Patrice grabbed my arm pulling me to her, trying her best to get me to hear her out, but I continued to walk, dragging all 5 feet 8 inches and 135 pounds with me. She didn't care who was watching and what they thought. Patrice was determined to keep me there and I was determined to find Maria.

"Terry, you are going to hear me out." Patrice screamed.

"I'm sure I will hear you out Patrice, but it will be done when I'm ready to."

It was clear I was a different man after the news that Dr. Wolciek gave me. I didn't care what was going on around me or who got in my way and I proved this by shoving JB out of my way who was blocking the door and trying his best to calm me down.

Natalie was trying to pull Patrice off of me and she was holding on for dear life while Natalie held on to her. I was like and NFL running back that defenders tried to bring down. Finally, I heard Patrice fall to the pavement of the hospital's entry way and my eagerness to find Maria kept me from looking back at anyone.

Chapter 33

It was a quiet ride back home and Patrice stared out the window with tears sprinting down her face as Natalie drove. She couldn't believe what happened back at the hospital and how quick Terry got so angry. Patrice knew for sure she was in love with Terry and she was willing to fight for him, but she only wanted to see some fight in him and not only a fight with Maria.

He wanted Maria and Patrice wanted her too, hell, even Natalie wanted a piece of her ass as well.

Patrice needed to tell Terry how they fell in love and why they loved each other. Receiving the news that a woman drugged him basically halted all of her plans.

"Trice' are you ok, you're kinda quiet over there girl?" Natalie asked.

"I'll be ok. Just get me home Natalie. If you have Maria's address and phone number, you can give me that."

"Come on now 'Trice. I thought you knew me better than that?" Natalie responded.

Patrice was confused. She thought Natalie would be the first to give her that information, but yet she seemed to finally be civilized about something.

"Trice, if you hadn't been staring out that window over there, you would have realized that I'm not taking you home."

"Natalie, I don't have time for all of this. Take me home. Please?" Patrice begged.

"No 'Trice. I'm taking you to Maria's house right dayumm now. It's time we put an end to this shit!"

Patrice was no longer looking out the window. Instead, she turned to look at Natalie and Patrice realized she was serious. Natalie felt the way Patrice did. Both of their eyes were filled with anger and they wanted Maria just about as much as a lion wanted his meal.

"Natalie? Are you serious?"

"Dead serious Patrice." Natalie said with a serious and blank stare on her face.

Patrice was ready to handle this with Maria, but she was worried because they didn't have a plan. No ideas about what was going to happen when they got there. No thoughts about what the consequences will be and that's where their personalities differ.

Natalie was the more go getter type, the risk taker, especially now. Patrice remembered her more as quiet and with a low self esteem. She told Patrice that Dr. T was responsible for this new type of Natalie and she couldn't say that she didn't like it. Patrice was more the type that has to have everything planned out and thought about.

She needed to know the who, what, when and where to something. Right now, for this situation, she was down for anything. This was the bitch that caused Patrice her man and Terry was not the type of man that came around every day.

She knew what she had in him and he knew what he had in her. Even though he was going through a lot right, Patrice was still going to fight for him.

Patrice just needed him to want his babygirl again and she needed for him to call her babygirl again.

Patrice was mad as hell and supposed to be getting in her bad girl mode along with Natalie, but she only had sex one time which didn't count because she was getting molested. Terry made her think thoughts she had never thought with another man before.

She imagined herself on top of his chocolate bar and his huge hands palming her breast like basketballs. The feel of her going up and down on his long and thick dick would put her in a sense of ecstasy; it would clear everything from her mind and allow her to be free. It would be simply impossible for Patrice to close her mouth, because it felt so damn good.

She thought about Terry bending her over and putting his entire dick inside her. He would penetrate to no end. He would kiss places that not only hasn't been kissed or touched, but it wasn't even discovered until the fullness of his lips parted ways and found them.

His tongue played mind games with her pussy as she thought my pussy had a mind of its own, but she was sadly mistaken because his dick and tongue would tell her to cum and she'd listen.

Patrice imagined Terry's strong hands pulling her towards him and while he shifted her sweaty hair to one side of her body, he would kiss and taste the other side of her neck. Only Terry could kiss her neck the way he did and make her ass jump. Then it would come time to suck his chocolate bar.

"Patrice! Patrice!! Hello?" Natalie screamed, snapping her out of it.

"Yea what is it?" She popped up like a kid sleeping in class and the teacher has just called her name.

"Girl, we are here. What are you daydreaming about?"

"Umm, I was just thinking about what I'm going to do when I get my hands on Maria."

Natalie parked the car down the street from Maria's house and tjey walked up to the front porch. A part of Patrice wanted to go back home and forget about it, but a better part of her was ready to hurt that bitch. It had to wait because Maria wasn't home so they went back to the car and waited like we were staking the joint out.

Having to wait was not a bad thing because it gave them time to figure out a plan and Patrice was excited about that, but Natalie was starting to get a little impatient so they talked as time went by.

"Trice, can I ask you something?"

"Yea, go ahead."

"Well, I know why I'm doing this, but why are you doing it? I mean, after what happened at the hospital today; I would expect you to say fuck it and go on bout yo' business."

"What can I say Natalie? I fell in love and I can't blame gravity for falling in love. I refuse to let Maria take love away from me. I lost my mom, I've lost my dad and I even lost you for a couple of years, but I'll be damn if I'm going to lose love. Not just any love, but Terry's love."

"What if he doesn't want that?"

"Then I love him enough to give him time to realize I'm the one he wants. We had real love before and he's going to realize that."

"Well 'Trice, from what I know about Dr. T, he's going to call and apologize for what happened earlier, he can't live with hurting anyone, no matter how bad they hurt him. He has to apologize for how he reacts. It's just in Dr. T to not want to hurt anyone and if he does, he feels horrible about it."

"So if he calls and apologizes, that means that he is treating me like one of his clients. I don't want Dr. T Nat' I want Terry."

"I guess that's how you will know if it's real with him. If he calls then its Dr. T and if he apologizes to you face to face then it's real love."

This was one time Patrice prayed Terry didn't call her. They talked for about another thirty minutes and Natalie spotted Maria pulling into her drive way. Patrice got nervous all over again because this was really happening and Natalie had to keep telling her to walk as if she's not looking to hurt somebody.

They finally made it up to her porch and Natalie was looking through some spotless windows to see if she spotted Maria.

"Do you see her Natalie?" Patrice asked nervously. Her legs shook uncontrollably and her heart was pounding hard as hell.

"Naw, not yet."

Natalie kept looking through the windows while hiding at the same time and Patrice stood right behind her, trying to stay out of the way.

"Shit 'Trice, I don't see her ass anywhere….."

"Freeze bitches, you hoes move and I'll blow your heads off." Maria screamed.

This was exactly why Patrice likes to have plans, not only plans, but good plans. Maria crept up on the and now they had a crazy bitch pointing a shotgun at them.

"Any one of you ladies would like to tell me why you are peeking through my window?"

Natalie and Patrice both were quiet. Maria looked at Patrice as if she wanted to hurt her bad and the feeling was mutual. Maria continued to point the shotgun at the ladies Natalie was itching to jump right at Maria.

"Natalie, how could you bring this bitch to my house? I thought we were best friends?"

"Best friends? I was your best friend until yo' ass went crazy over Dr. T. You didn't care about me anyways. You had the body and the money and you never made me forget that we were never equals. My sister is really in love with this man and I have her back no matter what."

"How do you know I don't really love Dr. T mami?"

"Because if you did, you wouldn't have put him up in the hospital and drugged him senseless, stupid ass!"

Only Natalie had the courage to curse somebody out and call them a stupid ass while they pointed a shotgun right at her.

"What are you talking about drugged him?" Maria said in a guilty tone.

"We know all about what you did to Terry, chica."

Natalie said, mimicking the way Maria talked.

"It's all on the cameras so it's only a matter of time before the cops come after you, so you might as well gon' turn yourself in!"

Fuck that, I don't want her to turn herself in, Patrice thought. She wanted to beat the shit out of her and then she can turn herself in. Patrice was standing there giving Natalie a look as if to say *'you are telling too much, shut the fuck up.'*

Natalie went on and on about everything from the hospital and the police knowing everything.

"Well mami, I guess since I'm already in deep shit, I can go ahead and finish you bitches off then huh?"

They walked into Maria's house with her still pointing the shotgun at them and she tied the two ladies up. She put tape over their mouths so they only had to think about beating the living shit out of Maria. They sat there not being able to do anything while Maria talked about what she was going to do to them.

Chapter 34
Terry

Something wasn't right and I felt it. I regret how I spoke to Patrice, but I knew that it was a totally different feeling than the one I was having. My heart felt like it moved, almost like something tugged at it. A small piece of Dr. T kicked in and I recognized the feeling.

It was the feeling I get when it's time to put my own shit on the back burner because someone is in need of me and being Dr. T, I had to know who it was. I went through my list of people and of course, Patrice was the first I called and it was to no success of mine. Then I tried Natalie, thinking that they had to be together, but Natalie didn't pick up either. JB was next on my list.

"Hello?"

"Yo' JB…." I screamed in a panic.

"Nigga you got some fuckin nerve to be calling me after you ran my ass over at the hospital." JB joked.

JB, have you heard from the girls?"

"Man, naw, my wife would kill my ass if she knew I was even talking to those women and I probably would…"

"JB, I need you to be serious man, fa real. I think something might be wrong with Patrice."

"What? You having a Dr. T's intuition or something?" JB joked again.

"Fuck it JB. I ran yo' ass over once at the hospital and if you don't get serious real soon, I don't have a problem with kicking yo' ass. Now get serious, shit!"

JB wasn't a bitch or nothing, but I just knew what to say to get him to get serious.

"Aight man, what's wrong with Patrice?"

"I don't know yet, but I definitely know something is not right!"

"So what do you wanna do man, you know I'm down for whatever."

I really didn't know what to do, but since I knew that Patrice was my heart, I figured I would listen to my heart and it would lead me straight to Patrice.

"JB, I'm on my way to come pick you up and by the time I get there, I will know where we're headed."

"Aight man, see you when you get here."

I hung up with JB and threw my Iphone in the passenger seat and began blaming myself if something had happened to Patrice.

I should have let her tell me what she had to tell me, but instead, I was stubborn. It was at this very moment, I remembered I loved Patrice. She was my life, she was the reason I lived and she was the reason I fought my way back from that coma.

I no longer gave a damn about anyone or anything, but Patrice. I clearly remembered the times we spent together. I thought about how I would watch her when she didn't know it and the times I kissed her, loving the taste of her lips while my tongue begged for the sensation of hers.

I remembered how we were not lazy with our love, we didn't blow kisses to one another because we realized how important it was to feel the other's lips. When I held Patrice, I held on tight as if it was my last night and her skin appreciated my efforts and repaid me by inviting me to touch her more and more.

Her skin was as soft as the softest cloud and was made just for me, a man with a rough exterior. We were so different which made us so right. She was my other half. What I lacked, she had and what I possessed the strongest were her weakest qualities.

I finally arrived at JB's house and he was waiting for me outside, with his head down.

"Damn nigga, were you speeding?"

"Shit yea, I got business to take care of." I said with complete subtleness in my voice that always scared JB.

"So, where are we going anyway Terry?"

"Maria's!"

"Damn, I finally get to see this fine Latino bitch huh?"

"You can see her all you want, but if she hurt Patrice or Natalie, she better take off running when she sees me!"

"Terry, what's makes you think she's over there?"

"JB, if your wife thought another chick not only was the reason you was in the hospital, but drugged you also, where do you think she would be right now?"

"Shit, you know my wife is gangsta, so I know she would be trying to kill that bitch man!"

JB tried his best to calm me down by making jokes, but my lips couldn't pretend to crack a smile just like my heart couldn't pretend to not love Patrice. I needed to know she was ok before anything else mattered.

"Aight man, seriously. After the way you did Patrice back at the hospital, why do you think she would go and defend you?"

I didn't answer JB, but a man knows his woman and a woman knows her man. One heart knew his mate by the way it would beat. Patrice knew I was in a bad space and I only had on my mind what she had on hers. Maria.

"I just hope you ready for whatever." JB muttered.

"What do you mean by that?"

"I mean, I hope you left Dr. T ass at home. It's time to get yo' woman, so I hope Terry is ready for whatever!"

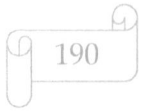

JB was right. I was ready for whatever and I've already called the police and told them when to come out to Maria's place.

We pulled up to Maria's house and JB took his time getting out, but I was halfway up to the porch. I signaled for JB to hurry his ass up because I was ready.

"JB, I'm going to knock on the door as if nothing is wrong and once I get in there, I want you to stay out here, looking through this window, and here."

I handed JB my gun. I didn't need it to handle Maria.

I walked up to the door and rung her door bell. I was nervous, but it was an impatient nervous. I was ready to have Patrice in my arms.

"Papi, what are you doing here?" Maria screamed with nervous excitement as she opened the door.

"Damn girl, you look sexy. Shit. I came over here to drop off this package for you and I know you know what the package is!" Maria squirmed at the thought of what it could be.

"Mmm, Dr. T, but you don't have anything in your hands!"

"That's because this delivery don't require me to use my hands!"

"Shit Papi, you know you can't be talking to me like that. Why didn't you call?"

"Because I'm running this show, I'm the captain of this ship and you know that already. Are you gonna let me in or do you want me to go deliver my package somewhere else baby?" Maria turned to look behind her and then turned to look at me again.

"Ummm, yea come on in."

"You ok babe, I mean, I knew you would be surprised, but you look like I'm interrupting something?" I walked in and gave Maria a kiss on her neck and she damn near buckled at the knees.

Everything in Maria's house was white and she always kept it clean except for today. I noticed dirty shoe tracks on her hardwood floors and there were more than one set of tracks. Now I was sure that

Natalie and Patrice were here, but I still played it cool until the time was right.

"I'm ok papi; you just caught me off guard, that's all."

Maria said fumbling over her words. She knew I knew something, but her pride wouldn't let her give in.

"Come sit next to me baby." Maria came and she walked fast and hard.

"Naw naw naw, slow that shit down. I just love to watch you walk and shift that ass from side to side. Good girl, I'm glad to see that you still follow my directions." Maria sat down right next to me and she didn't realize that she was falling right into my trap.

"Do you think you know me baby?"

"Of course Dr. T."

"Do you know what I would do to someone if they hurt me?"

My mood quickly changed and I was going in for the kill. My eyes had fire in them and I was no longer pretending to be Dr. T. I tried in vain to keep my fist from tensing up and slugging Maria.

"Uhhh, yea I guess so." Maria stuttered. I placed my arms around Maria. She thought I was doing it to get close to her, but she soon find out that she was wrong.

"Well let me explain it to you. I hate being hurt intentionally, but yet, people still insist to intentionally hurt me. So from now on, I'm no longer allowing people to hurt me. If they do, I'm going to do some hurting. Please don't let me find out they are hurting someone close to me either, I swear to......."

Maria tried her best to jump out of my arms, but I held on tight. I tried to squeeze the shit out of her. Literally squeeze the shit of her.

"Dr. T, you are hurting me, let me go." Maria screamed.

"I told you that if someone hurt me, I'm going to start doing the hurting. You almost killed me Maria and you drugged me while I was in the hospital. More than that, yo' stupid ass is trying to hurt my Patrice.

Where is she?" Maria tried to answer, but what I heard trying to come out of her mouth wasn't the right start to the answer I wanted so I squeezed harder.

Maria tried her best to tell me that she didn't know, but I wasn't accepting anything unless it was the answer to where Patrice and Natalie were. I stood up and brought Maria up with me.

"Where the fuck are the girls Maria? Tell me now! If you don't, I'm gon' throw yo' ass across this damn room, then I'm going to clean up those shoe tracks up with yo' ass!"

I held Maria by her throat and demanded she answer my questions. She hung in my hands while tears jump from her eyes in pain and she knew she had fucked with the wrong somebody. Maria begged that I put her down, but the only way she was leaving my hands was when she answered my questions.

I threw Maria over her table and she landed on the couch and I ran after her, grabbing and chocking her again.

"Do you want me to throw yo' ass again bitch cuz I don't have a problem doing it again?"

JB busted up in through the door and demanded I calm down. I gave him a look that said, mutha fucka you gon' be next if you fuck with me.

"JB, take yo' ass and go look for the girls!" JB went with no questions asked. I was on a mission and that was to make sure Patrice and Natalie were ok.

After a couple more minutes of throwing Maria around, my heart sank when I saw a shotgun lying on the stairs.

I knew for sure that she had done something to Patrice and Natalie, only I didn't know what. I ran to pick up the shotgun and rage came across my face as I pointed it at Maria.

"Did you kill them?" I asked.

Maria couldn't answer because I beat the shit out of her. I couldn't care less about me beating up on this woman. I think it should be an exception to the rule that a man shouldn't hit a woman, unless she tries to kill him and kill the love of his life.

Maria squirmed in pain and she was no longer this gorgeous woman with a nice body. She was dead to me and I didn't care if I was the one to kill her.

There she was panting for air, crawling across the cold hardwood floors with her bloody hands while I pointed her own shotgun at her. I demanded she answered my questions, she tried to but the only thing that spilled out of her mouth was the blood that I caused from throwing her ass back and forth across the room.

"Terry wait! Don't shoot her, I'm ok!"
Patrice came running from one of the back rooms.

She ran and jumped in my arms and I felt my heart beating again. She quickly jumped out of them and ran to kick Maria right under her chin, spilling out more blood.

"I told you not to fuck with me bitch!"

Maria was lying there unconscious while Natalie and JB were in the living room rubbing my fingerprints off of the shotgun.

Patrice and I were glued together, not wanting to ever be apart again. She apologized to me and I apologized back. We kissed like there was no tomorrow, like there was no next second, min, hour or day.

"I love you Patrice, I always have and I always will. I may have lost memory of that, but real, true love will always make you remember. I also want to apologize to you right here, face to face for everything that happened at the hospital."

Patrice held her hands in mine slammed her head into my chest, not wanting to reveal that she was crying. Patrice was my world and I realized that if I couldn't love Patrice or have her, I wasn't capable of loving or having anything. Our love was like the sun, it shined bright and even when it's time for it to not shine, and all the clouds, rain, sleet, and snow gets in the way of it, it can still shine bright.

"I love you too Terry and I wasn't going to give up on you babe. Now can I tell you how we fell in love? I just love thinking about that story."

Patrice looked at me with her beautiful hazel eyes and I had to resist them. I didn't need her to tell me.

"No Patrice, I know how we fell in love. I really do babygirl."

"How do you know Terry?"

"Well, I allowed my heart to open up and listen to your heart. Although there were times that we were not happy with each other and didn't speak, our hearts always stayed in contact, all I had to do was listen to my heart and it told me that you loved me."

"And my heart told me that you loved me too Terry. Terry I still have the envelope that the police wanted you to have, do you want to read it."

"No Patrice, nothing else matters now, I have everything I need right here with you babygirl. I love you." Patrice and I were walking into the living room to join Natalie and JB and there was Maria holding up the shotgun that JB had left on the table. She pointed it right at Patrice when she saw us come in.

"Looks like I'm going to have the last laugh mami!" Maria said with blood still coming out of her mouth. She limped with pain and smiled with ease. Maria knew that she was in control of everything now and her eyes never left Patrice's body. Natalie was itching at the thought of jumping at Maria, but JB wisely held her away.

"I told you chica that Dr. T will always be mine and I meant that. I don't have a problem not having Dr. T, but I'll be damn if you gon' have him!"

Maria raised the shotgun up and aimed it right at Patrice, I had to think of something quick, but I didn't know what it was. Before I could figure anything out, one shot to the head changed my life forever.

I watched as her body became wilted with death and she fell right onto the glass table and I knew that it was no more coming back from a shot to the head.

"Are you guys ok?" The policeman asked.

"Yes sir, we're glad you guys showed up when you did!"

"Well Mr. Davis, thanks for calling us out here when you did."

The police rushed to make sure Maria was dead and she was. Patrice stood there, frozen still.

"Terry, when did you call them?"

"It doesn't matter. Maria will no longer bother us ever again."

We all walked out together, lucky to be alive. Natalie drove JB back home while me and Patrice drove off with her falling asleep on me. I watched her and smiled to myself not believing what this one woman did.

Chapter 35
Terry

A whole year had passed since Maria's death. Patrice and I haven't spent a day apart since then and it was obvious that our love was real.

Everyone was influenced by us, even JB and his wife had gotten closer because of our love. Natalie snagged her a basketball star in Jeffery Pryor and they are now inseparable.

Patrice and I couldn't be torn apart from each other once moved in with me. I love how we wake up together every morning and fall asleep the same way every night. With her lying in my arms so our hearts could feel each other's heart beat.

Every night I kissed her angelic lips with mine just enough that my lips barely graced hers and I'll rub her smooth body until she was in la-la land.

I continued to write my Patrice poetry and she received one from me every week in a different form. I may have it delivered to her job with flowers or I may place it in the seat of her car with a Hershey's kiss placed on top of it.

For my next one, I had a special plan in place and I've been working on it for a long time. The following morning, we both got ready for work and I couldn't believe how beautiful this woman was to me.

"Good morning babe." Patrice whispered to me.

"Good morning babygirl, how did you sleep?"

"Come on Terry, I slept like a baby. Do you still have to ask me that every morning? You are the only person that knows how to touch me and when to touch me. I go to heaven every night when I'm lying in your arms." Patrice said as she kissed me and my lips danced when hers parted from mine.

"Baby there's some breakfast ready for you on the stove and I'll talk to you later."

Patrice ran out of door in a hurry and for once I wasn't too concerned with breakfast. I had a surprise waiting for Patrice when she cranked her car up.

Every day before sundown and every day after
Every day before sundown, I come here looking for you
Starring far out into the lake for only a love so true Like a visit from a rain drop, once I touch you, my life is done
Only I am your every rain drop, so I come back until your love is what I've won
Every day before sundown, I search for the grace of your walk and the power of your touch
Everyday day after, I gaze at your footprints and use the goose bumps you gave like a crutch
You are the color of air and have passion as your scent
You are no mistake my love, you're exactly what heaven meant
And every day before sundown, I'll come here in search of my kiss
And every day after, I'll see the shooting stars and make my wish
Kissing you and loving you will be the love we make
Wanting you and having you while the sun sets over the lake I can see you, come to me, run to me, faster and faster And finally, I make love to love, Every day before sundown and Every day after
I love you babygirl, you are my world and the reason I live life
Can you forever stay in my world and do me the honor of being my wife

I recited this poem over some jazz music and had it put on a CD so when Patrice cranked her car up

this was what she heard. I saw Patrice jump out of her car and run back into the house.

"Terry…what was that…I mean it was…are you serious?"

Patrice came in the house yelling for me and there I was, kneeling in the same suit I had on when I met Patrice at Shania's. I kneeled there and Patrice stood jumping up and down while tears flooded her beautiful, caramel skin.

I loved this woman hard and it wasn't how I made love to all those other women, in fact, Patrice and I haven't been sexually intimate, but we definitely, definitely made love. I didn't need to have sex with Patrice for us to make love.

I loved her and she loved me and I was sure that when I experienced the sweetness of her exuberant moistened garden while she experienced the stiffness of my renaissance manhood, we would fall in love over and over again. I had four roses and they all signified something.

"Patrice, the last words your mom spoke was for me to take care of you and that's exactly what I plan to do, babygirl I love you. Here is a rose that represents our past and everything that we've been through and here is rose that represents the love that you and I have together right now, the present. Baby these last two roses are special to me."

I couldn't stop the tears that were now trickling down my face as I thought about everything that has occurred since this beautiful woman had entered my life. I looked Patrice in her eyes and hers were filled with tears also.

Her eyes were glossy with what I wanted to be anticipation and she shook nervously as I spoke. The last two roses I gave Patrice were a red and white rose entwined together that communicated 'marry me.'

I placed a 2.5 ct princess cut engagement ring on the end of the stem and presented it to Patrice. I wiped my tears and halfway stood to wipe hers away also.

"Patrice, babygirl, I love you and I can't see my life going on without you. Baby will you marry me?"

While I waited on Patrice's answer for what seemed like an eternity, someone banged at my door and I look up. It was Brittany and Tren from Shania's.

ABOUT THE AUTHOR

Torey has been writing for about 20 years. His writing journey started as a freshman while doing a project in English class. It was then when he figured out what he wanted to do. Torey's burning pen started and has not stopped 15 years later, he enjoys writing about Love, Romance, Sex and really anything that crosses his mind or heart. He also broke into the novel world, writing his first novel "Dr. T Chronicles: Ocular Deception" which can be purchased under the "Order books" tab, along with his poetry book "Love Rescue."

Torey resides in Plano, Tx with the love of his life, Shelba Irving, whom he says, has made his writing 100x better. She inspires him and keeps him going. They have 2 beautiful girls and 1 handsome son, Londyn, Anaya and Kyngston and they enjoy just making each other happy. Many people want to know what inspires Torey. It's been mentioned that he just loves to know that a woman feels great about herself and loves to see women smiling. Through his writing, he hopes to give women an escape, if only for a moment, he hopes to leave an imprint through his writing to make women feel and know how special they are and they should expect to be treated like the queens that they are.

Torey Irving can be reached by:

Email: passioninkpublishing@gmail.com

Website: www.passioninkpub.com

Enjoy Dr. T's Nightcaps

More than what's Expected!

Everything is so much better when you don't use what's expected. For example if you use more than your hands to touch someone, more than the physical to touch someone, more than your eyes to see someone, more than your ears to listen to someone. Only thing that will work when expected is using your heart to love someone and sometimes you need more than that.

Mental Orgasm

Her eyes were closed as I entered inside her while making both of her knees buckle simultaneously. I touched her with the tips of my fingers and breathed erotic breaths into her ear that left her gasping and panting. Taking my hand, lifting her chin up to me, I tasted her caramel flesh, and she reacted by melting in my hand and tossing out orgasmic moans. She finally opened her eyes and realized, I never physically touched her, in fact, all I said was baby I love you. Mental Orgasm!!

I'm Determined

There's a song in my heart and I'm determined to sing it To you every day for a lifetime
There's poetry in my love and I'm determined to make you Say it in different genres, that you're mine There's love in my heart and I'm determined to make sure You have every ounce of it
There's passion in my eyes and I'm determined to let you Know those passionate eyes are only for you
There's determination in my mind to make you my wife and I'm determined to show you my determination in making That Happen, I'm Determined!!!!

Mentally Tasting your Heart

I am in love with your heart babygirl And I'm in love with knowing you are my world I thrust physically into your moistened essence And mentally into your emotional presence I fall in love in the journey that we are about to start And I am in love with you and is close to mentally tasting your heart!

Comfortable Heart

You know you are in love when you are in bed and your love says "Baby are you comfortable" and your reply is "yea, baby go to sleep. I love you" Meanwhile your arm is asleep, your neck has a vicious crook in it, and your back is somewhere you're not, but still you didn't lie because your heart is as comfortable as it can get.

Love Tears

I thrive on your Love tears and I use your Love Tears to take away your fears. They come in the moment of passion and ecstasy. While the long lasting pleasure of my nature waters your garden, your Love Tears covers your face and continues to make my nature harden.

My Rose

You are my rose and I will water you daily with love, shower you daily with affection and you will sprout and bloom with joy and the impatience for more.

Relax

Relax, breathe, exhale, inhale......Just enjoy the ways I taste your love with my tongue and make you explode and don't worry about the mess; I know how to clean up after myself.

Renaissance Manhood

I was sure that when I experienced the sweetness of her exuberant moistened garden while she experienced the stiffness of my renaissance manhood, we would fall in love over and over again.

Proper Kiss

Dr. T kissed places that only he knew wasn't kissed properly on her and she repaid him by quenching his thirst with the sweet pouring rain that only his tongue could produce.

Erotic Vibrations

Allow me to taste every inch of you, and I will send waves of erotic vibrations through the mounds, peaks and valleys of your body.

Swimming in your Essence

Allow me to go swimming in your ocean and I will come up drenched from the sweetness of your essence, and the quintessence of the waves we make is of nothing that words can explain!!!

Exploring your Earth

Can I explore every continent of your earth and go deep sea diving, tasting your ocean, lakes and streams. I promise I will make you erupt like a volcano and I'll graze your body while you try to control your screams.

Every day before sundown and every day after

Every day before sundown, I come here looking for you
Starring far out into the lake for only a love so true
Like a visit from a rain drop, once I touch you, my life is done
Only I am your every rain drop, so I come back until your love is what I've won
Every day before sundown, I search for the grace of your walk and the power of your touch
Everyday day after, I gaze at your footprints and use the goose bumps you gave like a crutch
You are the color of air and have passion as your scent
You are no mistake my love, you're exactly what heaven meant
And every day before sundown, I'll come here in search of my kiss
And every day after, I'll see the shooting stars and make my wish

Kissing you and loving you will be the love we make
Wanting you and having you while the sun sets over the
lake I can see you, come to me, run to me, faster and
faster And finally, I make love to love, Every day
before sundown and Every day after

Design of a Heart

We are truly the design of a heart. We started
out at a point, you went your way with your heart and I
went mine, but eventually we made it around the curves
and found each other, in love with one another, because
we met in the middle of each other's heart

It's Time!!!

It's time, close your mouth, roll your eyes back
to me and feel me penetrate. Feel my nature grow and
part through your gardens of love. I feel you rain on my
nature and in turn, I water your garden, while planting
my seed

Love Climax

Can I touch in a way that makes your body beg
for more throughout the day? Can I make love to you in
only a way that love would climax? Can your love
climax on top of my love and enjoy reproduction when
my mini loves travels through your streams of erotic
emotions? Understand, I only want to love your love,
nothing more, nothing less. I want to speak to you and
your love. Not only speak, but speak truths and facts.
Just trust me when I say, I only want to make your
Love Climax

Deathless.....Breathless....

I love your mind and your body, I make love to
it deathless and I seduce your mind and body until it
climax leaving you breathless. I'm willing to climb the
highest mountain, swim the longest seas and drift inside
the oceans that make your love. I'm willing to fall
victim to your grace and hope that we will together
mount up as one, leaving neither helpless. I am willing
to love you deathless until the day and beyond when
God leaves me Breathless

You're Speechless....

I ask how your day went only because if you give me an answer, it's my job to make you breathless and leave you panting in ecstasy. How was your day baby.......you're speechless

Deep Sea Diving

I want to go deep sea diving inside of your ocean and rise up drenched in your essence, heart racing, tongue dragging, panting for more baby.

At the Same Time

I love you, I want to make love to you, I want to make love to your love and I want you and your heart to climax simultaneously.

Comfortable Heart

You know you are in love when you are in bed and your love says "baby are you comfortable" and your reply is "yea baby, go to sleep" meanwhile your arm is asleep, your neck has a crook in it, and your back is somewhere you're not, but still you didn't lie because your heart is as comfortable as it can get.

Just not Enough

I look at you, you are so beautiful, I always dreamed of something so strong yet delicate; please wake me so I can see you again. You in my dreams are simply not enough

In Love

I am in love with your heart babygirl. I thrust slowly but surely and each time, I fall in love with you all over again because I am just that close to physically feeling your heart. I am in love with your heart babygirl And I'm in love with knowing you are my world I thrust physically into your essence And mentally into your emotional presence I fall in love in the journey we are about to start I am love with you and I'm close to mentally tasting your heart.

Your Essence

May your essence cloud my brain and my infatuation of thy heart will never strain. Could your love support my addiction
to be loved and may my love cure you from a broken heart?

There's a Song in my Heart

There's a song in my heart and I'm determined to sing it to you for a lifetime. There's poetry in my love and I'm determined to make you say in different ways, that you're mine. There's love in my heart and I'm determined to make sure you have every ounce of it. There's passion in my eyes and I'm determined to let you know those passion filled eyes are only for you. There's determination in my mind to make you my wife and I'm determined to let you that I'm determined to make that happen!

Open Arms

Our love greets each other always with open arms, promise me and I'll promise you to never close our arms of our love or we would find that we would only be holding ourselves!!!

In my open arms
Will be a place for your emotional storms Visit often and use anytime at your disposal And I promise to give your heart a Love proposal In my open arms
I will keep you from all harms
And wrap you up in my power And allow the rains of my love become your shower Together we can weather all storms While I protect you here in my forever open arms.

Resting in your Heavens

I am in love with you, I rest with you and am at peace with our love. I am home now, resting in Your heavens I lay with you, pray with you and graze inside your love. I am roaming around inside your Heavens
I wake up to you, lay next to you and cry with you. I lay in our bed lying in your bed of your Heavens.

I have walked away, came back and walked away plenty of times but as I kneel here before you, I have come back only to always, forever and a day Rest in Your Heavens.

How Our Love Sing

When our love sings to each other, the crescendo of our song dazes me in the perfect world. I am L.U.I Loving Under the Influence of your moistened essence. I am drawn vibratefully into our love waves. If only our love could sing, it would sing the ooooh's and ahhh's of Love. My falsetto love would make you feel like nothing ever dreamed of. And the different key strokes of your heart make me mmmm and ahh baby into ecstasy. Making you the maestro of my heart, directing my expressions and how they come to be. If only we could teach our Love to sing. We would sing in a new world together and enjoy the pleasure it brings. I would sing to your garden and make it rain its notes back on me. And together as a duet we would sit back while you enjoy the motions of my seeds. If only I could sit back and enjoy the things that our love brings into the essence of our expressions, we show How our Love Sing

Our Worlds

I have feasted from your garden, drank from your well of love and now I'm ready to spread my seeds inside your universe and watch our worlds come together!! Can I explore every continent of your earth and go deep sea diving, tasting your ocean, lakes and streams. I promise I will make you erupt like a volcano and I'll graze your body while you try to control your screams

Is it Possible?

Is it possible to believe in something so much and dream about something so much that it bleeds from your soul when it's not possible? I can't help but think about constantly telling you that I love you. More than

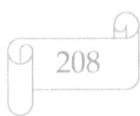

love could possibly love. I want to make your heart glow with love and passion for an eternity. I have searched and found love's heaven inside your essence and serenity and I will not, shall not let it waver in the spoils of solitude. You are my world and I never imagined missing someone before I even gone. You are simply my everything!

A New 24

It was a lovely 24 wasn't it. Goodbye to you my darling, I have a whole new experience to enjoy. New sunshine's, new clouds and new rains. Never will I feast or wallow in the spoils of your presence. Its time I leave you behind and leave our presence together in the past. Yea, sure I woke up to you and I was grateful, I also lay down ...with and woke up to a new. So don't pout or bitch and moan, just let me enjoy new adventures of what's ahead. It was an ok 24, but time is up, and honestly, I've had better and I'm looking forward to better. When I last saw you, I knew it was over because I kept waiting, looking at my watch anxiously waiting.... A new 24

I am In Love Again!

There's a panic in the air, trouble high in the clouds. Embers burn from yesterdays fires. A lost love buried beneath the rubble, but still there's life, still there's love, still there's......a want to go on, a need to keep going. There less panic in the air and suddenly clouds are disappearing, but still rain escapes the sky and falls upon my heart where she used to be, but thunderstorms become my heartbeat and lightning becomes my fuel, my adrenaline to keep searching, to keep loving the thought of love and to keep dreaming about you until you come true. Finally the panic has escaped the air, clouds and rain are in the afterthought and the only embers that burn is the fire that I have for you, the passion I provide when dreaming you and loving you into existence. I enjoy the panic-less air, the impatient clouds and the evaporated rain drops. I am in love again

The Music I Make
    Slowly walks up to the stage
Relishing in the moment just before snapping fingers
are raised
Kangol hat covering my eyes
Trying desperately not to see, but imagining a
wonderful surprise
Shades covering my nervous sight
And the mic is held firm and anxiously tight A sip of
Brandy traveling smooth into my body I speak into the
mic and enjoy how your moans got me Allowing the
slow hard bass of my voice to send your emotions into
flight
Hey Love, can I be you music tonight Can I rhythm and
blues my way inside you and enjoy your lyrics of
mmms and ahhs baby
Or can my instrument play inside your orchestra and
make smooth melodies of moans baby
I'll watch your body squirm to the rhythm of my voice
and watch your garden moisten in a daze Enjoy the
concert I give while I'm performing a tasteful soul
Love ballad inside your_____ (drops mic, exits stage)

Your Love
    Your love is my vision during the day and my
dreams at night, the loss of your love will bring about
blindness to my life and nightmares to my heart, Your
Love! I need your Love! Before my life could ever
begin to start

RnB of you Mmm's and Ahh's
    Through the rhythm of your mmm's and the
blues in your ahh's, my hands indented themselves onto
your thighs. My nature parted through remnants of your
soul and into your heavens and earths, while love
colored moans escaped your breath, passion tears hung
from your eyelids and your juices make for one hell of
an adult beverage that I can't pass up. I drink from your

well and become intoxicated instantly, and instantly I'm sobered through the rhythm of your mmm's and the blues in your ahh's

Eternal Fires

My love for you burns like embers from eternal fires, it will burn for eternity and never waver. As God gave us his Son, the love He gave wasn't in me to stay, love is only love when you give it away. My love for you burns like embers from eternal fires, it will burn for eternity and never waver.

In Love With our Silent Times

I'm in love with our silent times. The most beautiful and eloquent silence is that of two mouths, two lips, two souls, two hearts meeting in a kiss. I'm in love with our silent times!!

You're My World

It was not my body you touched, it was my heart. Not my ears in which you whispered into, it was our future you whispered into existence. It was not my lips in which you kissed, it was my soul. And it was not only you I made love to, I made love to your essence which is my universe and my world, you're my world!

Open Arms

Our love greets each other always with open arms, promise me and I'll promise you to never close our arms of our love or we would find that we would only be holding ourselves.

Lazy Kisses

People who throw or blow kisses are hopelessly lazy, why miss out on the softness and power in the feel of your lover's lips. My lips on hers can tell her anything better than being delivered through air or even through stumbling words.

Our Hearts

Only time can tell if my love for you can stand the test of time, but I don't need time to tell me that I am in love with you.

Only time can tell if my love for you can stand the test of time
Only your heart can beat in perfect harmony with mine
I don't need time to tell me that I'm in love with you All I need is for our hearts to keep doing what they do Breathe, love, kiss and beat together And hold on tight with every change of weather I won't accept the notion of that's it's too soon for this, too soon for that love
But I will accept the constant pleading of my heart when it tells what its dreaming of
The want to beat for a lifetime beside you The need to marinate for eternity inside you The have to be the rhythm's of you blues And the joy of the perfect I love you too's
Only time can tell if my love for you can stand the test of time, but I don't need time to tell me that I am in love with you

Warmth of Your Heart

I only want to soak in your ocean of love and try for a lifetime to dry off with the warmth of your heart
I only want to soak in your ocean of love with nothing pulling us apart
And try for a lifetime to dry off with the warmth of your heart
Not worrying about coming up for air, no panting or gasping for breath
No needing more than I have here, no more and no less
My only source of survival is floating in the waves of your love
While dreaming and wishing that others get the love I know of
My conscience is free while the moonlight shines over your essence
Which allows me drift far out and enjoy the seas of your presence
I only want to soak in your ocean of love and try for a lifetime to dry off with the warmth of your heart

Torey Irving